T0157579

A Change of
HEART

BOOK ONE OF A TRILOGY

ADRIAN DE NITTIS

BALBOA.
PRESS

A DIVISION OF HAY HOUSE

Balboa Press books may be ordered through booksellers or by contacting:

Balboa Press
A Division of Hay House
1663 Liberty Drive
Bloomington, IN 47403
www.balboapress.com.au
1 (877) 407-4847

Because of the dynamic nature of the Internet, any web addresses or
links contained in this book may have changed since publication and may
no longer be valid. The views expressed in this work are solely those
of the author and do not necessarily reflect the views of the publisher,
and the publisher hereby disclaims any responsibility for them.

The author of this book does not dispense medical advice or prescribe the use
of any technique as a form of treatment for physical, emotional, or medical
problems without the advice of a physician, either directly or indirectly. The
intent of the author is only to offer information of a general nature to help
you in your quest for emotional and spiritual well-being. In the event you use
any of the information in this book for yourself, which is your constitutional
right, the author and the publisher assume no responsibility for your actions.

Artwork by Sam Poidomani

Print information available on the last page.

ISBN: 978-1-5043-0625-6 (sc)
ISBN: 978-1-5043-0626-3 (e)

Balboa Press rev. date: 01/20/2017

ACKNOWLEDGEMENT

$\mathcal{L}$ike to say thanks to Kristy Jude and James for putting up with the constant sounds of every press of every key on the keyboard. Thanks to the talented Sam Poidomani for bringing this story to life through the design and creation of the cover art.

CHAPTER 1

An introduction

What if you encountered a chance in life that was far too electrifying to ignore? So you ignorantly went ahead and did it. Everything about it felt right, everything worked out, and it all fell into place perfectly. As time slowly went by, people were hurt, and you finally realised how wrong it actually was. Loved ones had forgiven you, yet it eats at you and consumes you in a way where it affects your daily routines, affects your moods, and makes you feel sick to the stomach. What if you were never able to forgive yourself? How far would you go?

CHAPTER 2

Notice the Signs

In the dark of the night, a sedan cruises down a main street at a smooth, comfortable speed. The air is clear, and the temperature in the vehicle is adequate. The lighting on the dashboard and the head tuner are both unlit due to a faulty circuit. The visibility in the vehicle is minimal; there are no streetlights to be seen anywhere. In turn, the individuals in the vehicle are practically indistinguishable.

In this dark environment, the poor lighting reveals only a silhouette of woman's hands gripped tightly to the steering wheel. With a deep breath of the cosy interior air and a mind flooded with many different thoughts, she looks towards the passenger seat. There sits a man who is staring out the windscreen into the nothingness of what's ahead. She smiles at his deep gaze into the abyss and then redirects her focus back on the road.

"Mum?" a little girl in the back-seat interrupts whilst glancing at the advertisements outside the car.

"Yes, Claire?" she answers, looking at Claire in the rear-view mirror.

"What do these signs mean? 'Call help lifeline'?" the

seven-year-old asks. Claire's twin brother, Joel, then looks to Claire as she raises herself up off the seat to get her mum's attention.

"Well, honey, a help line is a phone number that you call if you feel sad or angry or sick, and you need someone to talk to. The people you speak to help make you feel better. They are like doctors," she responds whilst still gazing through the rear-view mirror.

"But what happens if they can't help you, Mummy?" asks Joel.

"Well, people take different measures if they cannot be helped."

"What's *measures* mean, Mummy?" asks Claire.

"They try something else if the lifeline doesn't help them."

"Is that what Daddy did—take measles?" Joel asks.

She giggles at her son's mistake in pronunciation as she holds back her tears.

"But Mummy, you said Daddy was sick. If he was sick, you should have called them for him. They could have made him feel better."

The mother sheds a tear in her right eye. She slightly bows her head whilst keeping her eyes on the road. Interrupting her teary moment is a fast-moving vehicle hurtling past her, startling her. Once she regains focus, she replies, "Claire, Daddy never showed that he was sick. Mummy never knew that Daddy was sick. If I did, I would have tried helping Daddy myself." She bursts out in tears and bawls. She then covers her face and turns her head to the right, away from view of the children. With her right hand, she aggressively bangs the steering wheel.

"Mummy?" Joel says.

She wipes her tears, composes herself the best she can, and answers, "Yes, Joel?"

"I wish Daddy had called these help people. I wish Daddy was here with us."

"Yeah, Mummy. I wish Daddy was coming to watch me dance," Claire says sorrowfully.

She cries louder, finding it harder to compose herself. "Babies, Daddy is always watching us. Daddy is always looking after us and will always protect us. I want you both to remember that," she says, switching her gaze to the vacant passenger seat beside her.

CHAPTER 3

The Narrator

Hi, readers. Please allow me to introduce myself. I am the narrator of this story. You don't need to know my name, and it's completely irrelevant to you anyway; you may call me whatever you like. I will be explaining to you exactly how the scenes in this story happen. You may think my presence is not required for the story, but the author wanted me in it, to add something new to your experience.

This story is in real time. How cool is that? Anyhow, bear with me, and I hope you enjoy my narrating.

CHAPTER 4

One Chance

A small sedan parks on the curb in front of a local bar called the Lava Lounge. Established in 2001, the bar has been booming since its opening. Thirteen years later, not only is the bar a home for the locals, but it is also the must-go-to bar when visiting this city. All ages, faces, shapes, and sizes fill this fashionable place.

"Stanley Craig!" he says as he glances at the front of a closed envelope. He turns the envelope around and reads aloud. "The Lava Lounge, Stoke Street, Caulfield, 10:35 p.m." He then clicks the home button on his iPhone to spot the time: 10:20 p.m. With a letter opener sitting on his centre console, he slices the envelope open and removes a small, folded piece of paper. He then unfolds it to reveal a photo of a young man with dark, wet-styled brown hair; blue eyes; and baby-face features. He swipes his iPhone to bring up the camera and then places the paper on his lap to take a snapshot of the person's face.

The description underneath the photo reads:

> Name—Stanley Craig
>
> Gender—Male
>
> Age—23
>
> Confrontation—You must signal him with your index finger pointing up to the ceiling, like you have created a relationship with a waitress who has been serving you all night. He will notice you as soon as you walk into the bar. Upon entering, he should be sitting on your left. Keep your phone visible to match the photo you took with Stanley Craig's face. Follow Stanley Craig's orders once you are confronted by him.
>
> Good luck, Wethers.

He gives a quick press of the menu button for a time check. The phone reads 10:33 p.m.

"Okay, that's me. It's time to do this," he says, exiting the vehicle in a composed manner.

Wethers looks to the name of the bar flashing in neon lights above the entrance door. He walks around the rear of the vehicle and then clicks a button on his remote to open the boot. As it opens, resting on its own in the centre of the boot is a black briefcase. He rests the palms of his hands over the briefcase momentarily and then closes the boot. A simple click of a button on his remote fully locks the vehicle. After removing the phone from out of his pocket, he swipes to unlock and brings up the picture of Stanley Craig. While still holding the phone in his palm, he walks to the entrance door. The security guard nods his head to greet him and then opens the door for him.

Upon entering the Lava Lounge, his first view is of a large fountain with orange lighting in the midst of the streaming water. It is a beauty to look at and is something that everyone notices as soon as they enter. The next view is of a blonde waitress around 165 centimetres tall. She has a very pretty face and is behind the bar, mixing someone's drink. She looks and smiles at him as he walks in, but Wethers keeps his head down. To his left, he spots Stanley sitting at the bar with a brunette who looks to be in her early twenties; she seems to be enjoying Stanley's company.

"He was supposed to be alone!" Wethers mutters under his breath.

The brunette is resting her hand on top of Stanley's. Stanley then removes the brunette's hand and reaches for his phone inside his pocket. He clicks the menu button to note the time and then quickly looks to the entrance of the bar. Wethers's index finger goes up. Stanley acknowledges him and then motions back with his index finger. He whispers secretively into the brunette's ear and hops off the stool he was occupying.

Upon confrontation, Stanley offers his hand to Wethers, which Wethers happily accepts. Stanley swiftly moves towards Wethers's ear and says, "Mate, I'm not ready yet!"

In aggravation, Wethers hurriedly pulls away from

Stanley. He shakes his head and moves in towards him to reply, "This is a one-chance offer! When I'm gone, I won't be back."

With a sense of determination, Stanley responds, "I just met this beautiful girl at the bar, mate." He points his finger in her direction. "I just need a couple of hours, maybe three at the most. Come on, friend. Can you do this for me?"

With an irritated look, Wethers answers, "It seems to me that you don't really want to do this. I can walk away right now and never see you again. I'm totally okay with that. It's better for me and a lot better for you. These things happen all the time. It's great when my client has a change of heart."

Stanley places his hand on Wethers's chest and replies, "You don't understand. I *really* want this! I've thought about this over and over. I guess I just want a night of passion. No! Not passion. You see, this girl relates to me. She is something I have needed in my life for so long now. She is the missing link. The person I could open my heart up to. The person that actually cares about what I'm saying. She listens to me. I met her here last week, and we spoke all night, and that was it. We happened to meet again tonight. What are the odds, right? And that was without any organization or exchange of phone numbers. But I do still want this. I need you to do this for me."

Wethers looks to the brunette.

Stanley continues. "I really need to use the restroom, man. Can you give me five minutes?"

Wethers nods and makes his way towards the bar. He leans on the bar rail and looks down at the wet mat coaster running through the length of the bench.

The brunette looks to him and places her hand on his

bicep to get his attention. Wethers looks to her. She moves in closer to him and says with a soft voice, "Is everything okay with Stanley?"

He irately responds, "Yes, fine."

"Are you a friend of his?" she continues,

"Not quite"

"Oh, okay. Well, you see, Stanley and I have really connected. He intrigues me. I haven't met anyone like him before."

Just by that short conversation, Wethers had a feeling that she was in need of someone as much as Stanley was. He offers his hand to her. "My name is James."

She offers hers back and replies, "Hi, James. I'm Danielle. Pleased to meet you." They shake hands, and seconds later Stanley intrudes as he places his hand over Danielle's shoulder.

Wethers looks at Danielle and screams over the loud music, "Danielle, it's been a pleasure." He then walks to the entrance door.

Stanley looks to Wethers as he heads toward the door, and he says to Danielle, "I'll be back!" While holding his index finger vertically, he adds, "One sec!" He walks hastily to Wethers and places his hand on his shoulder to stop him from walking out. "Are we still good for later on?"

"Yeah, we're good. Just enjoy your night." Wethers walks out the entrance door towards his vehicle. Stanley watches him walk out and then heads back to Danielle.

"Is everything okay, Stanley?"

"Yeah, everything is perfect," Stanley replies with a smile.

"Is James a friend of yours? He came across as a very strange person, but friendly …"

"James?" Stanley repeats, dumbfounded.

"Your friend James. The man who was just in here talking to you?"

"Oh, James!" He smiles. "Yes, he is strange, but he's a nice person. He's very supportive!"

CHAPTER 5

Phone Call at 11:15 a.m.

While sitting tranquilly in his vehicle with his phone to his ear, Wethers listens to the dial tone of the person on the other end of the line. After three sets of rings, a deep voice answers.

"Judging by this phone call, I'm assuming it didn't work out with Stanley Craig?"

"You are correct in your assumption."

"Was it a change of heart?"

"Not quite. He requested more time!"

"Was it a length where it exceeded our agreement?"

"That's correct."

"So I guess I will expect a phone call from Stanley sometime soon?"

"I'm not sure about that."

"Well, that's a lot better on all of us, then."

"Indeed. He met some woman, and she too was in need of someone. The signs were there; they will prevail."

"Okay. Well, I have an envelope for another client in my drop box. When you are ready, you can come get it."

"I will collect it in thirty minutes."

"Good luck, Wethers." The conversation ends there.

CHAPTER 6

Thirty-three Minutes Later

Are you sure you want to do this? It's so wrong, but feels so right. These people depend on me. These people ... they need me.

He bangs the steering wheel in his car with his right hand, knowing that to the left of him on the passenger seat sits another unopened envelope. He stares unkindly at it. He doesn't want it, but he needs to have it. He needs to open it up. He just can't seem to shift his hand to reach over and grab it. His mind is telling him to get it, but his brain isn't commanding his hand to grab it. *Just grab it!* he tells himself. After several deep breaths, he reaches over and finally grabs it. He turns it over and reads aloud, "Janey Lane." His trusty letter opener rests serviceably over his centre console, awaiting his repetitive slice.

He's an absolute expert at the slice of the envelope and does it cleanly, almost at a point where it looks like it's still unused. He pulls out the folded piece of paper and unfolds it to notice a young-looking girl. He halts in angst and then shakes his head. "No ... No, no, no. No bloody way." The girl is very pretty; she has shoulder-length red hair, of a light ginger hue. Her eyes are green, her lips are strawberry red, and she has a smile that could stop anybody in his tracks. The description reads:

> Name—Janey Lane
>
> Gender—Female
>
> Age—16
>
> Place—Clover Park, 104 Clover Rd., Huntingdale. 4:25 p.m. Tuesday, 4 April
>
> Confrontation—Client will be standing beside a very large tree in the far distance of the park. You will know the tree; it will stand out like the apple tree did to Adam and Eve. She will notice you when she sees you searching for her. When you approach her, she will walk ahead of you and then get into your car. You will take her to the destination she has chosen. Once you reach that destination, you must abide by her commands.
>
> Good luck, Wethers.

CHAPTER 7

A Phone Call at 8:56 a.m., Monday, 3 April

"Yes!"

"Wethers, Stanley called me."

"And …?"

"His exact words were, 'Please tell him I said thank you very much.'" They both shed a moment of silence, where both men felt as though they'd succeeded.

Wethers finally says, "That's great to hear."

"Indeed, it is. It always is when a change of heart is comprehended."

"Yes. I just wish that all clients will feel the same way."

"Certainly … The good thing is, you must have said or done something to make him change his thoughts."

"Hopefully I did."

"These things do happen, Wethers. That one phrase or sentence or look you can give to someone can actually make a big change, a big difference in someone's life. This is where people are meant to meet certain people, and are meant to be the person that they are, regardless of what's happened to them in the past. Everybody has a purpose in life, Wethers. This purpose is yours, my friend. Be the best at it and conquer it, and good will come your way."

"Thank you. I do think about my purpose in life all the time. Why am I here? Why do I suffer all the time? Why did I meet you? Why am I pursuing this new career that has fallen into my lap? My purpose must make a difference in people's lives. My intention is to follow the guidelines, but it always seems to steer in another direction—a direction where the change of heart falls into place."

"And that's what you really need. I know your guidelines are the purpose of what you are here for, to make it easier on the client, but if it's not meant to be, that's when it automatically falls into place and opens up a whole new perspective for them. Wethers, you're making a big difference. You're indeed helping someone so lonely, so depressed, so in need of someone like you. Someone who wants to talk to someone who will listen to them and understand them, even though you're not supposed to. At the end of the day, it's always their own decision; you simply help them make the right one. You are a God in the minds of a lot of people who are suffering. Don't you ever forget that."

"Again, I thank you. It's always a pleasure to converse with you, my friend,"

"Take care, Wethers. Goodbye."

CHAPTER 8

Janey Lane

At 4:20 p.m., he exits his vehicle and walks around the rear of the vehicle to pop open the boot. Hidden inside rests that same briefcase that is still unopened. Again he rest both palms on top of it, and soon after he shuts the boot. He looks up to the sky and notices the sun shining ever so brightly. Rays of sunlight beam off the worn-out, silver playground slides. The Adam and Eve tree stands strong, green, and tall in the far end of this crowded park. Standing firm in protection of the tree is Janey Lane, holding an iPhone in her hand. By her feet rests a sports bag. After she types her message on the phone, she notes the time on the phone and looks ahead of her. As she does, she notices the man approaching her.

"Miss Janey Lane?"

"Yep, that's my name—minus the miss, of course. To society I'm known as Laney, So please, call me Laney." She holds her hand out to him.

He accepts her friendly gesture and then smiles at her intellect. "Well, fortunately, I'm not society."

Smiling at his remark, she responds, "That's a relief!

I think I like the way you think." Wethers smiles as Jancy continues. "So, mister, you want to hear my story?"

He shakes his head and responds, "No, thank you! Are you not aware of the guidelines, Miss Lane?"

She stamps her foot to the floor and utters, "But how are you to help me, if I'm not to share my story with you?"

"I have a certain window by which I must abide. A change of heart is always welcome and accepted."

She shrugs her shoulders and replies, "I know about the change of heart crap. But I need you to listen to my story!"

"I'm sorry, Miss Lane, but you must now lead the way to the chosen destination."

Again she stamps her foot on the grassy floor. "Stop calling me Miss Lane! It's Lancy. Now, please say it." He laughs at her angst. As she continues to demand, "Say it!"

"Miss Lane, we must leave now."

She gathers her bag from the grassy floor and says, "Forget it. I'm leaving." She begins to walk away.

He loudly states, "You know, a change of heart is always welcome."

She stops in her tracks, turns around to face him, and then says, "Are you programmed to say that? It's not a change of heart. You're not helping me at all—you're just making things much worse."

"Have you not read the guidelines?" he asks.

She exhales a deep breath of air in annoyance. "I don't care about your stupid guidelines. Everything always has to have guidelines. I just want to tell you my story!" She wipes a falling tear from her eye. "Can't you just hear my bloody story?"

After observing the ground beneath him in thought, he looks up to the blue sky to notice the sun shining ever so brightly. Enduring an act of kindness, he says, "What a fine day it is, Miss Lane."

She halts suddenly and shrugs her shoulders in sorrow. "Yeah, I guess it is 'fine.'" She says in mockery whilst air quoting.

"Would you like to join me back over there at that beautiful Adam and Eve tree?" he asks, pointing in the direction of the tree.

"The Adam and Eve tree?" she states, watching him smirk in disbelief.

"Yes. Look at how amazingly vast it is, and how it stands out. Hence the title: Adam and Eve tree."

Still smirking at his creative statement, she says, "It's funny how you call my tree the Adam and Eve tree. You see, I've been coming to this tree for years now. I actually love the fact you referred to it as the Adam and Eve tree, because this miraculous tree is very important to me. I've watched this tree grow, and I've watched people destroy it with their brutality in their markings." She points to a carved-out heart with "Jane loves Tommy" written into it. Wethers looks at the engraving, then looks at Jancy.

"Don't look at me! I'm Laney, and I've never heard of any Tommy before. Besides, I wouldn't ever harm this tree. This beautiful tree is my best friend; it has withstood nature's wrath on those stormy days, and yet it still blossoms every day of every year, just for me. It hears my cries, my fears, and my happiness. It's always here for me and doesn't judge me. Every day, I can come here to explain my day, and when

I'm done, a leaf falls for me right on my lap. It's become a common practice. It's true: it's showing me that it's crying for me; the leaf is its tear that I take away with me. It's the tree's way of telling me it is listening and it understands my pain. I'm relieved to see that you appreciate this tree as much as I do, mister. After so many years, I still haven't found the appropriate name for it … until today."

He smiles at her and responds, "I too have a place of sanctuary; it's not too far from where I live. It's beautiful, and the landscape is surrounded with pine trees and soft, luscious grass."

"Maybe you can take me there one day?"

While smiling at her, he replies, "Anyway, what will you call this miraculous tree?"

"I'll call him Adam," she says.

"Just Adam? Why not Eve?" he asks.

"Well, it's funny, because when you said Adam and Eve, it brought back a fond memory of when I was nine years old. I had a cousin named Adam; he was twenty years old. Adam looked after me and was always there for me. He took me wherever I needed or wanted to go. He went as far as sitting with me every time I called and needed him, and he helped me in so many ways when no one else was there for me. He would wipe my tears and then cuddle me until I fell asleep. You know the most important thing that Adam always did for me?"

"What's that?" he asks.

"Adam always listened to me. Do you know how rare it is to find someone who can actually stop, listen, and give 100 per cent focus on the recipient's plea? It's miraculous how it can help someone who is in desperate need of it. I loved my Adam so much …"

"Do you not speak with Adam anymore?"

"Unfortunately, no."

"Was it a family quarrel of some sort?"

"I wish it was," she says. "Adam passed away when I was ten years old. He was driving to my house to give me my birthday present, but he never made it. A drug- and alcohol-infused individual smashed into the side of his car, killing him instantly. The saddest part is I never got to say goodbye. To this day, I haven't gotten over it, and I don't think I ever will … But thanks to you mister, I've had Adam with me all this time, and I never realised he was right here by my side, protecting me. But I do have strong beliefs in things happening for a reason. Hence the title, the Adam and Eve tree."

"I'm truly sorry for your loss Lancy."

She says, "Hey, you called me Lancy. Yes! I win!" He chuckles as she pumps her fist by her side, so proud of her victory.

"You're a unique character indeed, Miss Lane." He attempts to seat himself on the green grass in front of the tree.

Before he is able to bend his knees, Jancy interrupts him. "No, wait!" She hastily searches around her bag, removing a picnic blanket. She then flicks it out to rest it on the green grass. After seating herself first, she looks to him and then invitingly slaps the floor directly beside her. "Take a seat, mister. I promise I won't bite." Her smile is captivating and so sincere that he smiles back at her, realising he is slowly developing a liking for this young girl the way he would feel for a daughter.

Seated beside her, he looks to the blanket and asks, "Do you always carry this picnic blanket around with you?"

She giggles and then responds, "Sure do. I told you I always sit by this tree. All by my lonesome, of course." She frowns. "I've even got some rice crackers in my bag. Here." She removes a packet of rice crackers from her bag, but a vibration in her pocket interrupts her gesture. After removing the phone from her pocket, she visibly holds the phone out for him to see. "He is so annoying." She then moves the phone closer in to him and adds, "Look at what he writes to me!"

His eyes switch from her pretty face to the screen of the phone as he reads. "Babe, I need to see you tonight. I want to make it up to you. Please."

She explains, "Okay, so that is Jacob. He is a complete and utter dipshit. (A) I'm not his babe, and I never will be. (B) He is just doing this because he lost a bet. And (C) the pig wants to get into my pants, even though he doesn't like me at all. The thing is, he has been texting me all day. I don't even know how he got my number. I'm just so over this." She aggressively types "Fuck you" and clicks send. "There. It's done!" she then places the phone beside her leg, in between the two of them.

After enduring a brief moment of silence, they both stare out into the open world, opening up their minds.

CHAPTER 9

The Narrator

Hi again. I am going to delve into their minds in one hit so you can see what they are thinking. I know—I love that idea too.

Wethers	Laney
I really want to help this young girl. I must be truthful to her and let her know that I really care about her feelings.	*I wonder what he is thinking? I still don't even know his name. I don't think he will tell me, though. Can I trust him, Adam? Is this man going to help me? I really need someone to help me. You know that, right, Adam? I need a sign, please. Please give me some sort of a sign …*
She has been through so much throughout her life. Honestly, I am afraid to hear her full story because I know I will be forced to take matters into my own hands, if needs be.	*Oh, no. He is still thinking. That can't be good.*
And this Jacob … The messaging just doesn't make any sense. I feel as though he really does like her but doesn't want to admit it to his friends.	

CHAPTER 10

Continued

$\mathcal{O}$nce the delving of their thoughts comes to a close, Lancy looks up to notice two leaves falling from the tree. She smiles and looks back down at Wethers, who is still staring into the distance.

"Hey, mister."

Wethers turns to face her. "Yes, Miss Lane?"

"Look up, quick." He does so almost instantaneously. Together they watch these two leaves falling in sync with each other. Once the leaves reach the height of their heads, they look forward into the distance to notice the leaves land in their laps. Together they turn to face each other, and Wethers offers his hand to Lancy. Lancy accepts it.

Wethers says with all his morality, "Hi, Miss Lane. My name is Tom Wethers."

She smiles, shakes his hand, and then replies, "Hi, Tom. Finally, it's a pleasure to meet you. My name is Jancy Lane, but society knows me as Lancy ..." While their hands shake up and down, she adds, "It's about bloody time, Tom. Now, will you hear my story?"

"Please," he says, chuckling uncontrollably. "Tell me ..."

CHAPTER 11

Laney's Story

"Okay so, I'm a fast speaker, If you miss anything, Tommy—" She halts to cover her mouth in amazement and then grabs Tom's hand to place it over the engraving on the tree.

"Tommy! Look! 'Jane loves Tommy.' What are the odds of that? I can't believe it."

They are completely awestruck from this coincidence, and Tom says, "That is a very big coincidence. Wow!"

Still overwhelmed, Laney says, "Wait a minute. Your name is really Tommy, isn't it? You're not pulling my leg, are you?"

Chuckling, he responds, "No, it's not Tommy!"

"Oh. I got really excited just then." She frowns.

"My name is Tom."

Her frown quickly flips to a smile as she replies, "It is Tom, then?"

"Yes, it's Tom, not Tommy."

She bursts out laughing and adds, "You crack me up, Tommy." Still smiling, she adds, "Anyway, I am way too young for you." She pauses. "Did I just say that out aloud?"

While giggling at her, he replies, "Say what? I didn't hear anything …"

"You're too kind. Okay, Tommy. Focus, will ya? Jeez. Anyway, what I want you to do, if I'm speaking way too fast for you, is to yell out, 'Lancy, slow the hell down!' Now, say it."

Laughing at her request, he enlightens her and responds, "Lancy, slow down!"

Shaking her head in distress, she yells, "No, do it properly."

Finally he says, "Okay, sorry. Lancy, slow the hell down!"

"Beautiful," she says, holding her palm out to high-five him. "Now, as you already know, Tommy, I am sixteen years of age, and if there is one weird fact about me that I should share with you right now, it's that as you can see with my hair …" She flicks either side of her hair with the back of her hands and then continues. "Ever since I could remember, I've always had one mirror in my bedroom at home. This mirror is the size of an A4 piece of paper. I cover this A4-sized mirror with a photo of Adam, about whom we previously spoke. I'm not one for mirrors, Tommy. A mirror is strictly for us to gaze at our doppelgangers. It doesn't show our true identity; it only shows us the character we try to be, just for society to accept us. Yep, that is correct, if you are wondering. You see, we cover our faces with chemically based pastes, and we do our absolute best to mask the uniqueness about us. Do you agree with me, Tommy?"

Tom stands there overwhelmed and stares at her.

She prompts, "It's okay, Tommy. You may respond."

Tom smirks at her charm. "I actually agree with you,

Laney. Every human being is a character that he invokes every morning to fit in with society. Very well spoken."

She administers one loud clap and then says, "Anyway, my parents broke up. I think about, I don't know … eighty years ago now. My mum is raising me on her own. My dad has completely disappeared, and not even God knows where he is."

Tom chuckles.

"It's true, Tom-Tom. I actually asked God, and he said to me, 'It's fine, Laney. You don't need him!" She used a deepened, robotic voice for God. Tom sits chuckling at her portrayal. "Thomas, focus, please. I'm being serious here!"

Still laughing uncontrollably at her humour, he taps his hand on her shoulder, trying to contain himself. "Okay, okay, I'm good. Please continue."

"So, while raising me on her own, she finds it impossible to spend time with me because she is always working. I don't see her, Tommy. I miss her, you know? I suppose she has to work, right? I mean, that's life. You've gotta go to work. Life is bullshit, Tom!"

He nods to agree with her. "You are correct in that proclamation, but you are only sixteen years old, Laney. You have a wonderful life ahead of you, and you have so much prospering to foresee in the future. You are a dazzling young girl. All I see for you is success."

She giggles timidly. "Are you some sort of a fortune teller?"

Tom chuckles at her query and answers, "No, not at all."

"But that's the part that baffles me, Tom-Tom. Why have I gotten to the point where I can't go on anymore and have taken that next step, speaking to you?"

"Because that is what you needed all along, Jancy! You needed someone to talk to—someone who was going to stop and listen to you."

"Like Adam did?"

"Yes, like Adam did."

After a brief moment of silence, Lancy has a recollection. "Hey, you want me to let you in on a little secret that not many people know about?"

"Sure!" he says, curious.

"Hold onto your butt, okay? This is really cool. A wise woman once told me that the universe is a great provider for all who believe in it. Now, I'm a big believer of anything you throw at me, Tom-Tom. But this? I really thought that this lady was crazy!" She twirls her index finger in a circular motion by the side of her head. "Anyway, this wise woman kept persisting and persisting and, last but not least, persisting. So what did I do? Well, as the naïve little girl that I am, I gave in. I believed her, Tommy. I actually believed this wise woman. And you know what happened, Thomas?"

Tom chuckled. "What happened, Jancy?"

"Hey," she says stamping her hand to the ground. "This isn't a joke, Mr. Thomas. I want you to take this shit seriously! Am I clear, young man?"

"Crystal!" he says, still chuckling.

"Well, I asked, and it bloody well provided for me. Did you get that, Thomas? You're quiet there. Am I moving too fast?"

He replies, "Yes, you are very clear. But in my head, I have three separate thoughts going on. Would you like me to share them with you?"

"Please! Share away," she says, motioning for him to move forward.

"Well, my first thought is how much you are making me laugh. You are one funny young girl, Jancy."

"Why, thank you, kind sir!" she says, bowing her head down and giving the same motion with her hand.

Trying to contain himself, he continues. "The second thought is, who is this 'wise woman' to whom you're referring? I mean, why aren't you branding her a name? Is this woman exclusive to society?"

"Actually, it's funny you ask this, Thomas. You see, this woman was just a friend whom I met through another friend. It's not important to reveal her identity to society, because they will make a mockery of her—as they do ever so cunningly. You don't need to know her name either, or even who she is or where she lives. It's none of my business, your business, or society's business. People always want to know everything, but this wise woman knows exactly who she is, and she knew that this day would come where I speak about her secret—and know to keep her identity a secret. It's a way for me to give back to the universe. Anyway, all I need to disclose to you today is the information I have about this wonderful universe. Now, Mr. Thomas, does that fulfil your second query?"

"Indeed, it does. Perfectly," he says, forming the letter *O* by making the tips of his index and thumb unite.

"So this leaves us with the third thought. Would you like to share this third thought?" she asks.

"Yes, most definitely. So the third and final thought is,

this provision that the universe has made for you—has it only been a one-off thing?"

She ignorantly shakes her head at his enquiry. "You didn't let me finish there, young Tom. That's why the third wasn't explained as yet. Be patient, young man. Good will come to all who are patient for it. Jeez, hasn't the universe taught you anything?"

Again he chuckles at her humour.

"Anyway, where was I? I've lost track now after I was so rudely interrupted. Not mentioning any names," she says pointing at Tom.

"This provision you asked about, Thomas. Well, it came within two days. I couldn't believe it. Was it a coincidence? Was it just pure luck? I didn't know at the time. Well, that's what was travelling through my mind, anyway. It was then that I said to myself, 'Laney, ask again. Ask for something that will be a miracle in my eyes.' So I did. I asked my ass off." With a smirk on her face, she shakes her head as she stares at the ground.

"What? What's the matter, Janey? It didn't happen, did it?"

She giggles at his question. "Thomas, my friend, I contest that query you have there, boy. It bloody happened, all right, and it startled the shit out of me."

"Really? What happened?" he asks in excitement.

"Well, I wasn't planning on disclosing the provisions I asked the universe for, but I guess I can say this one. You remember that guy Jacob on my message?"

"Yes, I do," he responds attentively.

"I asked the universe to make Jacob fall in love with me. Now, just so you are completely aware, Jacob hated me. The girls in his group kept teasing me, making my life as hard they could possibly make it. They tried to destroy me. I don't know why, because I haven't done anything wrong. I keep to myself and go through life on my own. But with these last few messages he sent me, it's actually quite scary!"

Beneath her leg, she feels another vibration, so she gathers her phone to see the notification. Before she is able to espy the screen, the screen goes black. She presses the home button and notices a notification for a message from Jacob. With her eyes wide open, she shows the notification to Tom.

"Swipe it," he suggests.

She does so and shows her phone to Tom. Then she reads out aloud, "'Hey, Laney. I'm so sorry I treated you that way. I wasn't in control of my own self. If that makes any sense.'" She giggles. "'You see, I cannot get you out of my head, Janey!' Oh, he called me Janey!" She places her hand over her mouth and continues. "'You think I want you for the wrong reasons, but in fact it's the opposite. I want to actually sit down and have a conversation with you. Maybe share a Coke together. Anyway, please reply back, Janey.'"

Laney and Tom gaze at one another in silence. Then she says, "Wow!"

"Janey, if I may speak? When I saw the previous message you showed me, I noticed the interest he had in you. Are you absolutely positive he hated you?"

"One hundred percent dead-on-balls positive, Thomas. He wouldn't even look at me at school. He was so caught up with how pretty he is and how popular he is. I never existed to him."

Together they smile. He says, "So what will you do, Janey?"

"What do you think I should do?" she asks.

"Well, how do you feel about this boy? From what I gather with the way he has treated you, you should damn well hate him. But the look on your face tells me otherwise."

"That look that tells you otherwise is precisely the true feelings I have for this boy. I have been in love with him for three and a half years now. I know it sounds crazy. And the fact that he hates me—very sad, I know. But the problem now is that I feel I forced this to happen. He only wants me because I asked the universe, and the universe made it happen. Will I be punished for this?"

"Why would you be punished, Jancy? You did nothing wrong. You asked the universe for something special to happen to you, and it provided it for you. I'm sure that if the universe didn't think it was right, it simply wouldn't give you this wish. Does that make sense? I don't want you beating yourself up about it."

"I won't beat myself up, Thomas. I already tried that several years back. It's pretty much impossible to physically do harm to oneself. Your mind simply won't allow you to do it."

He shakes his head at her statement and says, "Why did you try doing harm to yourself, Jancy?"

"I have my reasons, Thomas. Let me think ... For starters, I hate my hair, my eyes, my body, my nose, my face, and my mouth. I actually hate myself. I hate my mum for working all the time. I hate my dad for leaving us. I hate the person who killed my Adam. I hate the girls at school for teasing me. I hate that I fell in love with a boy who hates me. I hate that society is filled with judges. Everybody is a judge in this world. I'm so over everything ..."

Tom places his arm around Laney and pulls her into his chest.

She says, "And, did you know that you can actually purchase the lethal injection online? I just thought I'd share that with you."

He shakes his head in disappointment and replies, "Really? I wasn't aware of such a thing! It's actually quite frightening, when you think about it!"

"Indeed, it is!"

He holds her close in his arms. "Janey, I will start with this. Now, everything I say is always the truth—I won't say it if I don't mean it. You are a beautiful girl, Janey. I see no flaws with any part of your face, your body, or your hair. Absolutely nothing. You are very intelligent—actually, far too intelligent for your own good. You are the funniest, down-to-earth sixteen-year-old girl I have ever met. Adam is here with you, Janey. You're sitting in front of him, and you see him every time you come to this tree. He holds you and sheds tears with you. What you need to do is go home to your mum and tell her that you love her, and that you are thankful for everything she is doing for you. Tell her that you need to make certain days or times that you two can spend together. It'll happen if you make it happen, Janey. The girls at school will be jealous of you because the most attractive boy in school is in love with you. Janey, your life from this day will turn around for the better. The universe gave you what you asked because they knew you really needed it. Do you understand me, Janey?"

She momentarily pulls away from Tom's chest to wipe the tears from her face. Then, unintentionally kisses him on his cheek and says, "Loud and clear, Mr. Tom-Tom." Tom wipes the excess tears from off her cheek, and then Laney says, "Hey, Tom?" She halts, staring at the grassy floor. Then she continues. "I'm so happy I met you today, you know. You've made me realize how important it is to accept things as they come, and to look out for all of what the universe has to offer me." She recalls a past memory and adds, "Oh, hey. I need to tell you something."

He smiles and responds, "What's that, Jancy?"

Sitting with her legs crossed, she pats at her pants to remove excess dirt and dust. "You know how I spoke of the universe and its provisions, and also the wise woman?"

"Yes."

"Well, the wise woman expressed something to me about what will happen with you and me …"

In dismay, his eyes squint as he gazes at her. Then seconds later, his phone rings. As he reaches for the phone, he walks several meters away, holding his finger out to Laney and signalling for her to stay where she is. The number is known to him, and the time stuns him, revealing how late in the day it already is. He says, "Yes, my friend?"

"Hi, Wethers. How did you go with the client?"

His eyes search for Laney, and he notices her sitting by the tree with her phone in her hand. He responds, "I've progressed, I hope. I am still with the client now. I will keep in touch with her as days go by, just to make sure she is going to be fine."

"That's great news, Wethers, great news. In regards to this phone call, it's to inform you that I have a new client for you."

"That's fine! Please tell me it isn't a child or a teenager."

"Well, unfortunately it is indeed a teenager …"

"That's just great!" he grumbles.

"But unfortunately, there is a catch."

Wethers says, "What do you mean, a catch?"

"I don't want to disclose any details over the phone. Please check my drop box as soon as you can, and give me a call if you need to. You know I'll always be here."

"Okay, will do. Thank you, my friend." With a sense of doubt, he hangs up the phone and heads back to Lancy.

With his phone in his hand, and with time not favouring him at all, he stands firm in front of Lancy, observing how she remained seated by the tree.

Unexpectedly, she rises swiftly to embrace him. Tom happily accepts the embrace, whilst patting her back in a comforting manner. Once the embrace comes to a close, she lowers herself down till her toes touch the floor and says, "Tom, seeing as you noted the time on your phone and are still standing, I gather you need to leave?" She frowns.

"I do need to be elsewhere Janey. I'm truly sorry." Responding sorrowfully.

"I just need to speak with you, you know? About what the wise woman spoke of to me." She signals whilst pointing at her own chest. "Can you please come see me again?"

Tom chuckles slightly and then responds, "Have you not foreseen the future? I'm already here waiting for you, Janey. You simply haven't given me a time and date as yet."

With a sigh of relief and a great big smile, she embraces him firmly. "I was scared, Tom-Tom! I thought this was going to be the first and last time I would ever see you."

Smiling in glee, he answers, "Today was just one of many days where I will see you, Janey. That I promise you."

She fiddles with her phone and then unexpectedly offers it to Tom. Tom grabs it and looks at the screen to realise she has entered his name into her contacts: "Tom-Tom" as the first name, and "my best friend" as the surname.

"Go on, type in your number," she says with a playful smile.

He smiles back at her, surrenders, and types his number. Seconds later, he watches her again fiddling with the phone. Seconds after that, he hears a beep emerging from his pocket. As he grasps his phone, the number on the screen is unidentified until he swipes it to read. "Hi! It's Laney." He smiles and then saves the number in his contacts.

"Now, Janey, you have my number. If you feel sad or depressed, or if you need anything, you call me straight away."

"You are so sweet, Tom-Tom. I'm warning you now: you're going to get sick of me."

She laughs nervously, awaiting his response, and then he says, "That'll be impossible there, young Janey. Unfortunately, I must be on my way now. You call me whenever you feel you need to discuss anything."

Smiling with content, she responds, "Oh, I will definitely call you. Don't worry about that. And it'll be sooner rather than later, because we need to speak about that wise woman's words."

"That's fine. Just let me know." Again they embrace and then unexpectedly Laney kisses him on the cheek.

She watches him walk away, and he turns back with a

smile but keeps moving until he feels his phone vibrate again. He reads it.

"Hey, I wanted to say thank you again for everything you did for me. I love you, Tom-Tom—in a friendly way, not the tree engraving way."

CHAPTER 12

An Unexpected Phone Call

$\mathcal{A}$ couple hours after he leaves Laney at the tree, Tom drives to his next destination. The comforting sounds of Harry Connick Jr. play over the vehicles sound system. His phone rings, and the headset reads, "Simone calling." Instantly the name baffles him to a point where he is in two minds on whether he is going to respond. A greater force suddenly convinces him.

"Simone, how are you?"

"Tom, I'm okay, considering. What about you?" Her response is with a soft, weary voice.

"I must say I have had a splendid day—a day I haven't had for a very long time."

"That's good for you." From there, she surrenders to the silence of the conversation, awaiting a remark from Tom.

"So is everything okay?" he asks.

Her responses to him are swift and blunt. "Not quite, Tom. I really need to see you in person, as soon as you can."

"What is it regarding?"

"Like I said, I don't want to discuss this over the phone. When can you come over?"

"Well, I have a few more errands to run. How is later tonight, after 8:00 p.m.?"

"That'll be fine. I'll see you then. Thank you." Abruptly she disengages the call.

CHAPTER 13

The Drop Box

At 7:26 p.m., Tom sits in his vehicle, leaving it idling while he prepares himself for the next client; the information rests in that somewhat dreadful drop box. While he stares diligently at the box, two devil horns suddenly appear on either side of the box, with evil red eyes to accompany the horns. *I don't need to do this … I can just give it all up now, and not have that burden over my shoulders. It's actually that simple … But! I just cannot ignore this. As much as I dread it, I need to know and need to do this. I need to at least do this for Janey!* Abruptly, he opens the door and then heads to the drop box.

The envelope rests on the passenger seat of his car; the time on the head unit reads 7:47 p.m. He looks down at the envelope, trying to comprehend why every time he needs to open the envelope, it's always so hard for him. He nervously bangs the steering wheel of the car. After vigorously scratching his head, he turns to the clock on the head unit again: 7:51 p.m. "What am I doing? I've gotta go. I need to be at Simone's at eight. I'm not going to make it." He turns the ignition on and then presses the favourites button over the navigator to choose "Simone's Home." Upon clicking it, the navigator finds the quickest route there. A female voice says, "Your destination is seventeen kilometres away. The arrival time will be 8:12 p.m."

CHAPTER 14

Simone's Home

After pulling into the driveway of this two-story home, he places the gear into park and then looks at the time on the head unit, which reads 8:13 p.m. While staring intensely at the front door of this large home, his mind begins to decipher the reasons behind Simone urgently inviting him at such short notice.

While standing at front of the door, he forms a fist with his right hand and then knocks firmly but quietly over the centre of it. In a soft muffled voice, he hears, "Tom, is that you?"

Before he responds, he investigates the area, making sure he isn't visible to society. Then he replies, "Yes, it's me!"

Again the muffled voice replies, "Give me a sec. I need to put on something."

He shakes his head in disbelief, mumbling under his breath, "But she knew I was coming …"

Moments later, three different locks unlatch from this front door. Slowly the door opens to present a 175-cenimetre-tall brunette woman with a bob haircut that falls to her shoulders and big, beautiful hazel eyes. Before she opened the door, she asked for a second of his time to put something on, and all she could conjure up in that one second was a silky baby blue nightie with no tie to hold it closed. The base of the nightie stops just under the base of her panty bottom. No bra was protecting her breasts from being exposed. She's alluring, and he observes her whole body from head to toe, marvelling at what stands before him. After noticing this, Simone calmly closes her nightie to hide her privates whilst giving a cheeky grin.

"What's the matter, Tom? It's not like you haven't seen this before." She offers her hand to him and then walks him into the home.

Upon entering, he searches the lounge area, which was the first visible room in the house. Then he habitually gazes down to the vacant couch. He watches Simone head into the kitchen, and then he calls out, "Is Josh not home?"

Simone switches the kettle on from in the kitchen area, which he is able to see from where he stands. "I was just about to make myself a coffee before you knocked. You want one?"

Upon realizing he is being ignored, he decides to not mention Josh again. "Sure."

"One and a half, and lactose-free milk, yeah?"

"Just the one sugar now," he says, smirking at himself.

In the lounge area of this home, Tom seats himself at the far end of the three-seater sofa. He watches Simone walk into the room still wearing that partially closed nightie that has opened from the short gusts of wind generated when she is in walking motion. She's seated in a vulnerable matter, and he notices her breasts protrude from out of the nightie. As the noblemen he is, he lowers his head, and his eyes remain wide open, trying to battle the temptation. After placing both cups of coffee on the coasters, she sits herself down only inches away from him. He looks to her as she crosses her left leg over her right, to make herself comfortable, and she then finally covers her exposed parts again with her revealing nightie.

He takes a loud sip of coffee from his cup and then says to Simone, "It's nice. Thank you." A nod of her head is the only response offered. Then she too leans forward to grasp her cup of coffee, sipping it loudly. Cuddling the cup with both hands, she uses the emitting heat from the mug to warm her half-naked body, remaining nonverbal. He isn't sure about how to ask Simone why this invitation was so important to request at such short notice, so he sits there sipping his cup of coffee and hoping that soon she kicks it off.

Five long minutes of complete silence, with the continuous sound of sips every ten seconds or so, finally aggravates Tom. She notices the aggravation and asks, "What have you been doing with yourself, Tom?" She rests her coffee on the table.

"Not much. My new job is keeping me very busy, and it helps take my mind off a lot of things."

"Things? Things like me?"

He places his mug on the table before responding, "No! Not you … Past things." She grumpily nods her head. He senses Simone's anger and realises this is going to get out of hand very soon, so he knows it's time he step up and ask why he was invited over. "So what did you need to discuss?" he asks, sipping his last bit of coffee. Before he leans back in his seat, his phone unexpectedly beeps a message. His eyes open wide to watch Simone look to the modern clock that hangs on the wall, and he sees it is 9:26 p.m.—far too late to be receiving a text.

"Are you in some sort of a hurry?" she asks peculiarly. "Do you not like my company anymore?" She moves forward out of her comfort zone.

He senses hostility in her voice and responds, "Simone, I don't want to do this. I just want to know if everything is okay." Again his phone beeps twice.

Swiftly her comfortable position has vanished, and anxiety quickly takes charge. "Who is messaging you, Tom?"

He placidly removes his phone from his pocket. Once the screen lights up, he notices three notifications from Jancy. Avoiding her prying eyes, he tilts the screen somewhat so he can privately read it.

"Hey, Tom-Tom. I'm so happy I saw you today. I hope you can meet me again tomorrow? I know it's so soon, but I need to speak with you ASAP. You hearing me, Tom-Tom?" He gives a smile as he keeps reading. "I luvs you, Tom-Tom. Don't ever forget that. In a friendly way, of course—not the tree-engraving way!"

While tapping her foot on the floor, Simone asks, "Who's Jancy?"

"She is a very good friend of mine whom I just met today. She was in need of a close friend, and I want to be there for her. I need to be there for her."

"Really? What about me?"

While shaking his head at her remark, he responds, "Simone, I cannot do this! I'm sorry." Taking a stand, he attempts to head to the front entrance.

She grabs his bicep and begs, "I'm sorry, Tom. Please don't go." In an unexpected manner, she decides to throw her arms around his body to embrace him. This embrace is the tightest he has ever felt. "I really miss you, Tommy!"

His eyes raise at the fact she called him Tommy, and this one name brings back blissful memories. With a sudden sense of strength, she pushes him down to fall on the sofa. Upon landing, she seats herself comfortably on his lap. The sense of lust hurriedly fills up his adrenaline meter. Routinely, his hands find her waist to grasp it whilst his head bows in disarray. To make herself comfortable, she applies pressure against his pelvis, grinding into position. Immediately, she senses his penis fighting to free itself from his pants.

But Tom has other plans. He wants to keep it contained as much as he can. After exhaling deeply, he says, "Simone, we can't do this! I'm sorry—we just can't." Simone is kissing him on his lips, trying to keep him quiet, while she rubs his penis through his jeans. He's aware that he needs to fight this, and he carefully grabs each side of her biceps to pull her away from his face.

"Why, Tom?" she asks in aggravation. "Is it her?"

"What? Who? No way. Simone, you are not in the right frame of mind to do this."

"How do you know? How do you know if I'm in the right frame mind or not? You don't know what I've been through, sitting here waiting for you every day to arrive, and you never come. I'm convinced, Tom: you must hate me."

"No, Simone. That is not true."

"Well, what *is* true? Can you tell me the truth for once?" His phone beeps. "Yeah, there's my answer right there. Go, Tom. Go to your new girl." She hops off of him to sob as she lies in the foetal position.

While standing over her, he says, "Simone, I'm not going to leave with you thinking that I'm seeing someone. It's not what you're thinking; I specifically told you that Jancy is a friend in need of a friend, and I happened to land into her life. I will continue to be her friend as long as she needs me. So please get it out of your head that she is a girlfriend of some sort. I know what state you are in—I've seen it before, and I'm not taking advantage of it. You know me well enough, and I'm not that type of person." He adjusts his clothes and then makes his way to the door, adding, "I will check in on you tomorrow."

She remains foetal whilst quietly sobbing.

As soon as he slams the door shut in his vehicle, the first thing he thinks of doing is to tend to his busy phone. An unexpected message from Jancy sheds some excitement for him after experiencing something he never expected or desired. The message reads, "Hey, Tom-Tom, why aren't you replying to me? I really miss you. Is this a bad thing? I don't know—maybe you have ignited this spark in my life, where I want to see more of you. Need to see more of you. Am I really writing this? You probably think I'm crazy, Tom-Tom. Anyway, please message me back so I don't go to bed thinking that I lost you. P.S., I luvs you—not in the tree-engraving way"

Smiling enthusiastically at her message, he replies, "Hey, Jancy. Please forgive me; I was unable to tend to my phone. Yes, tomorrow will be fine. Give me a time, and I shall be there." Upon tapping send, he looks to the seat on the passenger side, reminding him of the new, unopened client that rests there. Unintentionally, he turns to face the windscreen to realise Simone has been watching him all this time. He shakes his head at himself and then drives off.

After six minutes of driving in the direction of his house, his phone beeps again. With excitement, he opens the screen, only to realise it is a message from Simone. The time reads 9:58 p.m. *Simone?* he says to himself. In curiosity, he swipes and reads.

"Tom, I really miss you, okay? I'm sorry I reacted that way. I hope you can find the time tomorrow to see me."

After releasing his anger over the steering wheel, he unexpectedly hears another beep. As he looks down at the phone, he notices a message from Jancy. He pulls the car over to open the message.

"Hey, Tom-Tom. You replied! Woohoo! You know I'm jumping up and down on my bed, pumping both fists in the air. Victory again! You made my night, Thomas. Oh, that's right—you wanted a time for tomorrow. Hmm, let me think! My index finger is over my lips. How does 1:00 p.m. sound at our tree? Let me know, and don't keep a girl waiting."

After inhaling the deepest of breaths, he ponders whether he go and see Jancy and ignore everyone else, but the anticipation of the envelope militantly calls upon him. His right hand holds the phone with the message from Lancy, and the left holds the envelope he is so eager to open. Debating on which is more important, he chooses his right hand, due to him being right handed and also favouring to choose Lancy's message. He responds, "Hey, 1:00 p.m. is fine. I'll see you back at the tree." He clicks send, noticing his phone beep again. In anguish, he finds it is from Simone.

'Tom, please don't ignore me. I just wanted to let you

know that I gotta go to the shopping centre tomorrow at around noon, after I finish work. I won't be home till 1:30 p.m. Do you think you could make it at that time?"

He smiles as he stares up to the roof of his car in search of God. "Are you serious?" he says. After giving his response some thought, he replies to Simone, "I'm not ignoring you. I will let you know tomorrow. I may not be able to make it at 1:30 p.m., but I'll let you know prior to that time."

As he clicks send, again his phone beeps, displaying a message from Lancy. He reads, "Luvs you, Tom-Tom."

He serenely continues his drive home.

CHAPTER 15

A Two-Bedroom Apartment

Tom pulls into the driveway of his apartment. A quick press of the green button on the remote resting on the centre console of his vehicle opens the garage door in front of him to reveal a two-car garage that has one side occupied with a little yellow hatchback.

By the door to the entrance into the home sits another remote that he uses to close the garage, watching it till it hits the bottom to lock it up.

It's 10:42 p.m., and he finds himself in a pitch-black apartment. He feels for a light switch by the door and hurriedly flicks it to light the room.

The apartment is of a cosy size, and the first piece of furniture presented to him is a rectangular dinner table that comfortably seats up to four people. Over the messy table, bills pens and papers are scattered throughout the whole of the table. To the right of him is the kitchen area, and he heads there to open up the fridge. From the fridge he removes a one-litre carton of lactose-free milk that was sitting right beside a carton of full cream dairy milk.

In the course of making himself a bowl of corn flakes, he

hears a toilet flush. Thinking nothing of it, he continues to enjoy his late-night dinner.

He has a congested mind, and all that happened today is circulating, trying to force itself out somehow. Using one of his many bills, he turns it over and grabs the pen with his vacant hand. He begins writing, "So I have to see Jancy at 1:00 p.m.," he mutters. "And Simone wants me there at 1:30. There is no way I'll make it to Simone's at 1:30. I'll need to tell her in the morning. I'm sure there was something else I needed to do tomorrow." He taps the base of the pen over the table, trying to recall. "Why can't I remember?" The tapping has somehow turned it into a tune … Whilst bopping his head to the beat he created, he senses someone behind him.

"What's got you thinking so deeply for you to tap out the 'Seven Nation Army'?"

Alarmed, he turns to where the voice appears from and replies, "Paise!" chuckling at her remark, he examines her so the readers can have a description. Paisley stands at 164 centimetres tall. She has wavy blonde hair, blue eyes, and a big, noticeable smile. Accompanying this is her black nightie that looks to be far too small for her body. Naturally, Tom marvels at Paisley's physique every time he sees her.

While resting her right hand on his shoulder, she pulls his head to her face to kiss him on his cheek. "You okay? I was concerned earlier as to why you weren't home yet." She seats herself down beside him and notices Tom tilting his head to the right, trying to relieve the niggling pain in his neck. "You got a sore neck?" she asks sympathetically. "Want me to massage it for you?"

He responds, "No, I'm fine, Paise! Just need to sort this out …"

She stands, places her hands on his shoulders, and attempts to massage him. Tom slowly turns his neck around as she massages, instantly recognising the relief she is conducting.

"You want me to make you a cup of coffee?" she asks whilst deeply manipulating his muscles.

"No, thanks. I had one earlier on tonight." The relief he feels somehow begins to arouse him.

"You seem a little distant, Tommy. I'm not sure I like this …" Suddenly she halts the soothing massage and turns his head to face her. After making herself comfortable over her seat, she caresses his hands, resting them on her lap. "Tell me now, mister: what is bugging you? I promise you we will not go to bed until you tell me."

"It's nothing, Paise. I just have a few appointments tomorrow, but they are so close in time, and I don't want to let either of them down … Oh, shit!"

"What! What is it?" she asks anxiously.

"The envelope—I left it in the car. I forgot all about it …"

Already off her seat, she intervenes. "Oh, I'll go get it for you."

"No, no … I don't want to open this envelope, Paise! I just have a bad feeling about it."

"But it's a client, Tom! What if they need your help?" His response expresses a look of sadness. She stands up off her chair, and says, "I'll get it for you, okay?"

As she attempts to walk towards the garage, Tom stops her and says, "I just need an endless cuddle from you."

She stops in her tracks and replies, "Oh, that's so beautiful. You know I love my cuddles … Come here."

As soon as their arms wrap around one another, they

hurriedly feel the absence they have been enduring all this time. The grasp is tight, and their hearts gently collide.

"Tommy?" she says warmly.

"Yeah, Paise?"

"I'm gonna go get this envelope, and we will both open it up together. Then we'll go straight to bed." She pulls away to smile at him. "This envelope is what's keeping you awake. What do you think? Does that sound enticing?"

He chuckles, fully releasing her. "Okay, but I'll go get it. It'll be far too cold for you right now."

"My nipples gave it away, didn't they?" she says, laughing at her witticism.

After three long minutes, Tom comes back into the house to find Paisley busy in the kitchen, making a tea for herself.

"Was it cold?" she asks.

"Not really," he responds. "My nipples aren't erect, are they?" Together they giggle.

"Are you sure you don't want a coffee? I mean, I'm here now, and I'm making a tea for myself. My offer still stands."

"No, I'm good, thanks."

Whilst preparing her tea, she notices Tom staring at the envelope, debating on whether he should open it. "Hey, Tommy," she calls out. "You want to open it together? I can sense you really don't want this one!"

He looks to her and smiles at her kind gesture. "You know me well, Paise! Why are you so nice to me?"

"Because I love ya, Tommy."

When they're seated together at the table, Paisley holds her mug with both hands while Tom rests his hands on the table and stares deeply at the unopened envelope. She inhales a deep breath and then grabs the envelope from the table. With her fingernail, she slices the top of the envelope to open it up.

"Why am I so afraid of opening this envelope?" he says feebly, pounding his hand against the table.

"Maybe it's because you have had enough of this. Or maybe you feel that you need to focus your time on Jancy?"

He shakes his head. "Well, that is what I've been thinking since I met with her today."

"Yeah, I know. Dad already informed me." She places her hand over his arm. "Listen, I'll open it and read it. When I'm done, I'll hand it to you! Okay?" She removes the paper from the envelope and notices no photo within the envelope. "Hey there's no photo in this one," she states obliviously. While still resting his head on the table, he manages to shake it at her remark.

Paisley continues to unfold the paper, and in her mind she reads the first name of the person. In immediate shock, she inhales sharply, and it's noticeable to Tom. "What the hell? Did Dad talk to you about this?"

He abruptly looks up at her noticing, the shudder in her voice. "Yes, he did. Why do you ask?"

"Well, ignore this one, Tommy. I'll talk to my dad tomorrow. You don't need this right now!"

He shakes his head in disbelief and says, "What do you mean, just ignore this? You can't expect me to ignore it, especially now that you are making such a fuss over it!"

She places the paper back into the envelope. "No, Tom! I'll speak to my dad and sort this out."

"Paisley, I don't want you getting involved with the clients that Brandon gives to me."

"Tom, you know I never do. But sometimes my dad doesn't think about what he does ... It's really late now. Let's just get you to bed." Knowing he is unable to win this argument, he wearily gives in to her demand. She adds, "I'll be there in a few minutes. Let me clean up, and I'll come lay with you."

He's already heading to his resting place, and he waves his hand in understanding.

Certain that Tom has left the premises, she looks to the clock, which reads 11:11 p.m. She searches through her favourites over her phone till she spots her dad in there. She presses it aggressively and waits for it to ring out.

The answering machine picks up and says, "Hi, you've called Brandon. Sorry I missed your call. Please leave a message."

"Dad! Are you serious, giving him Josh? I cannot believe you. You're lucky you didn't answer the phone—I was going to blast the shit out of you." She hangs up violently and then bangs the phone over the bench.

Ten minutes is all that she needs to clean up. Finally the lights retire, darkening the entire apartment. In the bedroom, Tom is facing the wall with his back to the door. She removes her nightie, wearing skimpy BONDS underwear and a sports bra. On the base of the bed is Tom's T-shirt, which she habitually throws over her half-naked body. Slowly she lifts the blanket to hop into the bed.

"Tom?" she whispers delicately.

"Yes, I'm still awake."

She giggles at his claim and says, "You want me to cuddle you? And I'll tell you about my day, to help you fall asleep?"

He grins. "Sure."

After moving in close to him, she places her arm around him, resting her hand over his stomach and managing to keep her body at least ten centimetres away from his. "Okay, so today, I caught up with Zoe. You remember Zoe, yeah?"

"Zoe was the movie fanatic?" he asks,

"Yep, that's Zoe. Anyway, we went to have lunch today at Café Qui, your favourite place. She said that you really need to watch this film … God, I can't remember what it was called, though." The heat from her body gradually creeps in closer to him. "I've got it! *Eternal Sunshine of the Spotless Mind?*"

"Yeah, with Jim Carey and Kate Winslet?"

She slaps his stomach with her hand. "Yes. She recommends you watch it."

"I've already seen it. Great film."

She slaps him, a little harder this time. "You've seen everything. You're no fun." From the constant shuffling and frolicking, she has now managed to press her entire body against his, spooning him. The warmth of her body and the idea of her against him hurriedly forms his erection. With her hand pressed against his exposed stomach, he fears she will lower her hand accidently, feeling his erection. He shuffles down a little to make her hand creep up to his chest.

"I'm supposed to be helping you sleep, and I'm sitting here asking you questions. How silly am I?" she says obliviously. In awkwardness, he turns his body over to lay on his stomach, doing all he can to hide his erection. But Paisley keeps following his movements, holding him closely.

Finally, she glides her fingers away from his stomach across the bare of his back. Then she soothingly tickles with her nails, noticing a shiver erupt from the wonderful sensation he is experiencing. From this one sensation, his erection slowly reduces, allowing his mind to focus on his slumber.

A minute later, she asks, "So tomorrow you're going to be a busy boy, aren't you?"

After several seconds, Tom hasn't responded. She realises it is time for her to follow suit and shut her eyes for the night, to enter into her own slumber.

CHAPTER 16

Not Such a Bright Start to the Morning

The sun rises, and Tom still lies in his bed, deep asleep. In the empty spot beside him, there sits the T-shirt Paisley wore, resting on a creased pillow. In the kitchen, Paisley stands by the stove dressed in her nightie whilst cooking bacon and eggs. Her phone rings loudly, disrupting her course of cooking. Groaning prominently, she hurriedly grabs the phone and places it on silent so as to not wake Tom. She reads the screen and callously responds, "Dad! What were you bloody thinking?"

"Honey, I wasn't sure what to do. I thought it over and over. You are well aware that I get the calls, and it wasn't just the one call—it's been several. My words aren't helping this client at all. This is why I'm sending the client to Tom."

"Client? Are you serious, Dad? This is how you refer to him? As a fucking client?"

"Well, Paisley, what do you expect me to do?"

"I want you to take care of this yourself, Dad. Don't give this 'client' to Tom."

They endure a moment of silence until he adds, "Has he left yet?"

"No!" she responds irately. "He is still in bed. I'm in the middle of making breakfast. This envelope, made it so hard for him to fall asleep, so I laid with him till he finally did."

"So how is it going, anyway?"

"How's what going, Dad?"

"With you and Tom?"

"I'd rather not go into that at this time. And besides, I need to wake him. He kept saying he has a busy day today."

"Okay, I'll speak to you later. Are we still doing dinner tonight?"

"I'm not sure. I've gotta wait to see what Tom says. I'll speak to you later. Goodbye, Dad." She drops the phone to the bench, which makes a loud sound, while she tries to tend to the burning eggs.

That one thud wakes Tom in a fright. He turns to notice Paisley isn't lying next to him. The time on his phone reads 9:31 a.m. After navigating into his messages, he presses on Simone's name and then types, "Simone, unfortunately I won't be able to make it at 1:30 p.m. today, I'll message you as soon as I know I can make it over."

CHAPTER 17

Adam and Eve Tree

Tom parks in the exact spot he did yesterday and notes the time: 12:51 p.m. He effortlessly spots the large tree in the far distance, and he squints to try to make out whether Laney rests by the base of it. The visibility from this distance is not quite sufficient, so he hurriedly heads towards the tree. As his vision becomes clearer, he realises she isn't there yet. Shrugging his shoulders in heartache, he continues there anyway.

After comfortably seating himself by the base of the tree, his mind wanders momentarily in wonder of where she could be. Suddenly he mutters under his breath, "Laney, where are you?"

A soft, distant voice responds, "I'm right here, Tom-Tom!"

It startles him, and he stands to search his surroundings, quizzing whether the voice was of a ghostly nature. He then says, "Laney, where are you?"

"I'm right here, Tom-Tom!" she replies in a soft, ghostly voice.

Tom knows something was up, and after a rapid probing of the environment, he walks around the enormous tree, to find Lancy standing there with a big smile on her face. Unashamedly, she jumps onto him, hoping he can carry her weight. He does so with ease and then embraces her as though they haven't seen one another for years.

"Tom-Tom!" she screams loudly. "You have no idea how happy I am that you came to meet me today. That devilish voice in my head was telling me these silly things, but I said, 'Listen, you little DV, I'm the one in control here. I ain't listening to your lies. So rack off, cos I know he will come! That's what I told that little devil."

After chuckling at her sense of humour, he asks, "DV?"

"Oh, sorry!" She laughs. "It stands for devil's voice!"

CHAPTER 18

The Narrator

Hey, readers. I'm sorry for interrupting this scene with Laney and Tom, but something major came up—something much more important, so important that I needed to stop everything else and share its importance with you.

CHAPTER 19

Harsh Words

"Mum, why didn't you tell me he was coming? You keep telling me he is coming back, but days and days go by, and he's never here. I think you're actually losing your mind. He doesn't give a shit about you—or about me. All he ever cared about was his stupid job …"

"Josh, that's not fair. Don't speak that way about him, please."

"Me, speak about him this way? Have you actually heard yourself, Mum? You think I don't hear when you speak to whomever the hell you're speaking to?"

She cries uncontrollably. Without any remorse, he continues his ranting.

"This is why I'm leaving. I don't wanna see you, him, or anyone. As far as I know, you and Dad are both dead to me. I'm packing my shit and leaving. I'll be gone by the time you wake up tomorrow." He walks away from her, stops by the hallway, and adds, "Oh, and just so you know, your bullshit counselling hasn't done shit for me. So all of you can go get fucked."

CHAPTER 20

Back to Laney and Tom

Seated in the same positions as they were yesterday, Laney is in deep thought, trying to pick the right words to say to Tom.

"So how has your day been, Laney?" he asks.

She inhales deeply and then exhales at a much quicker rate to prepare herself for the incoming explanation. "Well, this morning, I spoke to Mum!"

"Oh, well, that's progress. So how did you go with that?"

"Well, again she was in a rush to leave for work. I tried to fit in as much as I could, but she wasn't listening to me. It was making me nervous, and I was telling her to just stop and listen, but she wouldn't."

He puts his hand on her shoulder "Shh ... Janey, it's fine. Calm down, okay? Take deep breaths, in and out ... Tonight you need to speak to her. Tell her that you will set your alarm to wake up early enough for the both of you to sit and discuss your true feelings. The morning is when our minds are refreshed and crystal clear. What do you think?"

She throws herself onto him again, embracing the love she feels for him. His embrace is of the same nature, and she notices this and says, "Hey, Tom-Tom, do you feel that?" "Feel what, Jancy?"

"You know; like when you're acquainted with someone whom you have connected with in a way that you just feel safe. You feel that you are free to do, act, and say whatever you like to this person. And you know that everything else around you is irrelevant! It's non-existent. It's just you and the kindred connection you share with that unique soul. It feels wonderful. I'm surprised you don't feel this, Tom."

He smiles and responds, "I couldn't agree more with you, Jancy! That was very well spoken. Such a pleasant heart-warming statement, absolutely amazing … You know, it actually brought back a memory, a phrase a wise man once told me."

She interrupts. "Oh, you have a wise man, and I have a wise woman!" They laugh together.

He continues. Anyway, I never forgot what he told me. I actually noted it down, and studied it to the point where I remember it clearly. It went like this. 'True love is when no soul around you exists, except for the soul that it is united with.'"

She steps back in surprise, holds her hand to her heart, and says, "Wow! That is so deep." She types it into her phone, remembering each word as though she has heard it over and over again. After she types it in, she looks to the heavens, deep in thought. "Hey! That could work three ways, you know." Together they pause in silence,

"How do you mean?" he queries.

"Well, hear me out. This could cater for, like, a love at first sight scenario—you know, *Romeo and Juliet*. And …" She points her finger at him. "It could also cater for our scenario. The scenario that involves you and me, the friendly course of love. Well, I'm hoping it's friendly." She raises her eyes in trepidation. Tom raises his own. Before he is able to rebut the second scenario, she continues.

"And for the third and final scenario, I kind of picture a newborn who sees its mother for the first time. That is so beautiful, Tom-Tom. I really love it. I will always remember this. Can I ask who this wise man is? Does he have a name? Is he a man of mystery?"

He chuckles. "His surname was never mentioned in the little time I spoke with him, but when we shook hands, he called himself Adrian."

"Well, I would love to meet this Adrian."

"Unfortunately I haven't seen him since that day. In my heart, the innocence behind the reason I met him was the universe's doing, so I could hear his phrase. And today carries another purpose: it was for you to elaborate more on the phrase itself, to open up other definitions. All I saw in the phrase was that of expressing the *Romeo and Juliet* scenario. But you saw through that, and you opened up so much more out of it. You truly are a unique person, Janey." In an honest smile, he adds, "I can't help but marvel at the beautiful smile you carry."

She gives a smile, blushing.

Leisurely seated in silence, they admire the sounds of birds whistling, creating their own little song and harmonising amongst each other. The gusts of fresh air the tree provides allows for the tranquillity they both desire. With each breath they take, they understand and indulge the goodness of the fresh, unpolluted air the tree produces for them.

Having finally overcome the fear of conveying the news the wise woman spoke of she says, "Tom, do you recall the conversation you and I were meant to have in regards to the wise woman?"

"Oh, yes. Please tell me."

"Okay, so before I begin, I'm just telling you now that this woman knows her shit! Pardon my English. So what happened was she stated clearly to me that I was going to meet you one day. I didn't have any details on you—no name, and no mention on how handsome you'd look or how perfect your smile is." After waving her hands she adds, "I was told nothing! I guess I had it in the back of my mind and knew this day was coming. She did state how I was going to meet you, and the way we met was exactly how she relayed it to me. She explained it to a tee. Truly amazing shit."

In admiration, he responds, "That's fine. Go on …"

"Okay, so bear in mind that at the time, I thought this was so far-fetched, and I wasn't trusting it one bit. But she said to me the future shows a man. This man's job title labels him as the person who is going to help me, but instead of him helping me, he is going to be the one who needs help." He narrows his eyes in disbelief and remains quiet, so she continues. "I know this all sounds mind-boggling to you, but you need to hear me out. I'm not sure how I'm supposed to say this, Tom, but … it's about your boy."

"Josh? How do you know about Josh? I haven't seen Josh in a very long time."

Sensing the anger in his voice, she places her hand on

his thigh. "Tom, listen. Your son needs you. He needs you right now."

His phone suddenly beeps, disturbing her report. He grabs his phone to see a new message from Simone at 2:03 p.m. The message reads, "Tom, I need you to come home right now. It's really important. Please come home."

Laney reads the message and aptly says, "Tommy, your son—he needs you right now!"

He kisses her cheek, gives her a quick embrace, and storms off to his vehicle.

During the course of his journey, he responds to Simone's message. "I'm on my way." Moments later, his phone rings. The screen says it's Paise calling. He answers over the loudspeaker. "Paise, what's up?"

"Tommy, this envelope—you need to come get it now."

"Why? What is the rush all of a sudden?"

"Because you need to tend to this client immediately."

"I'm on my way to Simone's now. I don't think I'll have a chance to pop around."

"Well, I'll meet you at Simone's house. I'm just around the corner from hers."

"Okay." He abruptly ends the conversation.

Upon arrival, he finds Paisley's vehicle idling in the driveway of Simone's place whilst Simone stares diligently from the window of her home. He approaches Paisley's vehicle, embracing her as she exits the vehicle. In the midst of the embrace, she hands the envelope to him and then whispers in his ear, "Tom, you know I love you, yeah?"

He pulls away from the hug and whispers, "Paise, I want

you to go home. I don't want you being around here at this present time … And I love you too."

Before she is able to re-enter into her vehicle, Simone exits her home, screaming, "Where do you get the nerve to step foot on my property?"

Tom looks to Paisley, who has just entered into her vehicle. He says, "Paisley, go. Now!"

While pacing steadily towards Paisleys car, Simone says, "Yeah, Paisley—go back to where you came from!"

Tom places his arm against Simone's torso, stopping her from moving any farther towards the road. After watching her burst out in tears, he catches her limp body before it collapses to the floor. Holding all her weight in his arms, he places her body on the sofa in her home.

Still sobbing drastically, she announces, "Tom, it's your son, Josh. He needs you … We need you."

He notices the suffering she has been through. Then he remorsefully caresses her hair away from her face. "Where is he?" he asks softly.

Her eyes are far too droopy; she seems as though she cannot keep her weary eyes open. He begins thinking she has taken some sort of a sleeping pill, or she has had a week of sleepless nights. Due to other worries, he continues with why he has come over. "Simone, I need to know where Josh is."

While searching the room with her blurry eyes, she notices the envelope in Tom's hand and asks, "The envelope … What's in the envelope, Tommy?"

Having completely forgotten about the envelope, at first he gazes at it. Then he unfolds it to view the contents inside of it. Upon noticing the name of the client, he drops the paper to the floor beneath him, staring at paint on the wall in front of him. Without any hesitation, she gathers the paper from off the floor, reading out the name of the client.

"Josh Wethers … gender, male … aged fifteen years … what the hell is this, Tommy?"

"Where's Josh?" he screams. He dashes to Josh's bedroom, heavily thumping the door. With no reply, he thumps again, harder. He tries the handle to find it locked from the inside. In a furious manner, he steps back courageously and then smashes into the door at full force, knocking the door from off its hinges and watching the hinge buckle upon impact. He storms into the bedroom, to find Josh lying flat on the bed, dressed in jeans and a singlet while his arms hang flaccid over the edges of the bed.

"No!" he screams. "Simone, call the ambulance now!"

While lying on the sofa in a comatose state, Simone fails to hear Tom's scream. He places his ear to Josh's mouth and finds him still breathing. His head looks to the heavens, thanking God that his son is still alive.

His eyes suddenly wander around the room, spotting an opened bottle of pills resting on his bedside table. Upon gathering them, he notices some have been consumed. He leans into Josh, delicately whispering his son's name into his ear. Sensing Tom's warm breath against his cold skin, Josh's eyes open in flickers until they are able to finally focus on Tom standing by his bed.

"Dad!" he croaks loudly with sincerity.

CHAPTER 21

A Father-Son Reunion

With the two of them seated at the table in the kitchen, Tom observes Simone by the kettle, making a coffee.

"How long has it been, Dad?" Josh asks.

Tom shakes his head in disappointment. "Far too long, son." His eyes focus back on Simone to watch her shake her head in disappointment.

"Dad, all I wanted was a father who was going to be there for me … Do you have any idea what my life has been like without you? I mean, I'm not sure exactly what happened with you and Mum—and to tell you the truth, I don't really want to know. All I ask for now is to have you back as my dad. I mean, didn't it hurt you that you never saw your only son?"

"Josh, of course it did. I really struggled to get through my days on earth. I tried everything to fight off the thoughts about all the wrongs I committed. It wouldn't go away and kept getting worse. Nothing could help me, and I never wanted to listen to anyone. Your mum forgave me for all the wrongs I did, but it still wouldn't go away. That's why I had to leave."

Finally, Simone joins them on the table and seats herself

beside her son. While gazing at her in a comforting manner, Josh adds, "But I was only six years old, Dad."

After a sip of her coffee, Simone intervenes. "Five, sweetie."

"Five years old. You missed ten years of my life!"

Tom breaks out in tears whilst Josh remains seated as an onlooker. With a sudden sense of intimidation, Tom stands and says, "Son, I'm sorry. I cannot do this right now …"

Josh says, "Do *what* now, Dad? You see? That's the problem right there. You have done absolutely nothing for us. And you're gonna just get up and leave again?"

Tom slams his palm on the table. "Josh, I have my own ways of dealing with these situations. I know I'm in the wrong for everything, but if you don't give me the space I need right now, we will be back at the same position we were ten years ago."

Noticing his frustration, Simone says, "Sweetie, he is right, I pushed and pushed your dad so much, and look what happened: I lost him. We must let him deal with this in his own way, and he will be back. I know he will …" She gazes into his eyes and adds, "Am I right, Tom?"

With remorse, Tom nods his head in acknowledgement. Remaining unresponsive with a mind cluttered with thoughts of Laney, he shakes his head slightly, hoping Simone can get him out of this.

She says, "Let's give Dad space. Yeah, Tom?"

He nods in acknowledgement and adds, "Just please don't do anything silly, Josh."

Josh sighs in anguish. "Well, I won't kill myself, Dad, if that's what you're thinking. Trust me—I've already tried, and I figured out that your mind simply won't allow you to do it."

CHAPTER 22

Some Time to Think

$\mathcal{U}$pon the arrival at his place of sanctuary, Tom momentarily remains seated in the comfort of his vehicle. Visions of Josh lying lifeless in his bed frightens him to the point of punishing the steering wheel with the base of his fist. Lancy scatters his mind, effortlessly overpowering Simone and Josh.

From his vehicle, he stares through the window and into the grassy field where his resting spot is located. All that he wants is to contact Lancy, but he is completely aware that it is not the right thing to do. Again, the steering wheel becomes his new right of punishment.

Finally, he stops the brutal bashing of his steering wheel and heads out into the field to see if the fresh air can help his mind refocus.

CHAPTER 23

How Did You Know?

Tom eagerly sprints back to his vehicle, slams the door shut behind him, and then dials Laney through his Bluetooth. It rings once before Laney answers.

"Tom! Oh, God, are you okay? Is your son okay?"

"Janey, yes, he is fine. I am fine … Tell me, where you are?"

"I left Adam about ten minutes ago. I'm walking home now."

"Tell me your location?"

"Um, that is a great question. Actually, I'm not quite sure where I am, if that makes any sense, cos I do know where I am, I just don't know the name of the street.

He laughs. "Okay, well tell me a street name you can see."

"Um, let me see …" He can hear her breathing deeply while hastily trying to search for the street name. "It's called Coleman Street, Tom-Tom."

"Okay, I'm familiar with that. Wait at the end of the street, across from the big red home."

She laughs. "Tom, do you notice that house as well? That is so cute. Did you know that I stop in front of it all the time and just stare at it? The worst part is, the owners have caught me several times." She giggles at herself. "Do you know of someone who lives in this street, Tom-Tom?"

"No, Janey, I don't. I just happen to drive past it regularly."

"Okay, this is so exciting. Where abouts are you?"

He spots her standing by the red home and says, "If you turn around, you will see my vehicle slowly approaching."

She giggles as she turns around. "Yay! There's my Tom-Tom." Like a little girl, she jumps up and down, clapping her hands and almost dropping her phone to the floor. Through the windscreen of his vehicle, he perceives the excitement she is displaying. After catching her phone, she says, "Tom are you there?" She hears the sound of laughter.

He says, "I'm here, Janey. Hang up the phone and get in the car."

"Kay!"

Upon entering into the vehicle, she places her bag by her feet and then thoroughly examines the interior of his car. Tom notices this and sarcastically says, "Is my car not suited to your standards?"

She laughs and taps her hand on his thigh, trying to compose herself. "No way. Cars don't really faze me at all. I was actually checking what type of person you are."

"How do you mean?"

Leaving her hand on his thigh, she says, "Well, I noticed everything is neatly placed, with no food scraps or empty bottles scattered throughout the vehicle. It assures me you are a clean person. And Lancy loves a clean person."

Pleased with himself, he responds, "Well, that's good to know."

Finally, he gazes at her hand that rests comfortably on

his lap. Then he looks to her eyes to find them staring into his. A smile and a simple nod sends off the vibe to invite her hand to slowly move in the direction of his crotch. She gazes at him deeply, biting her bottom lip. With a sense of arousal, he signals to allow her to continue. Amazed that he let her be, she places her hand on his crotch, rubbing it through his pants and feeling his erection.

His head drops back against the head rest while he closes his eyes with desire. "Laney, we mustn't do this ..." he appeals.

Ignoring his plea, she continues her massage, realising it is time to offer him the relief for which he yearns. She delicately grabs hold of it to remove it from his pants. The prominence of his penis deeply excites her. She applies several strokes delicately as though it needs some attentive care. He hasn't felt this desire for a very long time now, so he is happy to leave her be. She lowers his pants to his knee and then spreads his legs slightly so his testicles have breathing space. She gives one last gaze into his eyes and then finally bends forward, placing her mouth around the head of his penis. He moans upon contact as she licks at the tip of the meatus like a lollipop. Lightly running her teeth over the shaft, she takes the length to penetrate deeper into her mouth.

Using her tongue, she tickles the rim of the meatus whilst moving up and down over the extent of it. He hasn't felt this desire in a long time, and he senses the ejaculation approaching at a rapid rate. Finally, he looks down at Laney to notice she has managed to take the whole of his penis deep into her mouth, hastily moving up and down on it. He senses it throbbing against her tonsils.

He's unable to contain it any longer, and he happily releases his ejaculate deep down her throat. Oblivious to the coming of his ejaculation, she unexpectedly feels it squirting to the back of her mouth and then down her throat. Not wanting to dirty anything around her, she holds the penis inside her mouth until she feels the throbbing ease to the point where it falls limp.

CHAPTER 24

The Narrator

*W*ow! I bet you never expected that saucy scene. I'm wondering, did you picture it the way I saw it? I bet you did; But in the reality of this story, that scene never actually took place! Yep—it was simply a tease the author and I came up with, to keep the reader observant. Anyway, where was I? This is what really took place ...

CHAPTER 25

Story Continues

*I*n deep thought, together they endure a moment of silence. Lancy uses this moment to ponder on how she will go about asking Tom about his son. She gazes at him whilst his mind is focussed on the landscape ahead of him. The courage in her heart suddenly peaks, allowing for her to finally ask, "Hey, Tom-Tom. I care about you! In saying this, I am wondering how it went with your son."

He exhales and responds, "I found him asleep in his bed, and I thought he may have overdosed until I checked his pulse. When I knew he was fine, I waited till he awoke from his slumber."

"Wow! That must've been so scary!"

"It was. Anyway, we hugged, and I found it to be a hug that I was longing for."

"I'm just curious—how old is he?"

"Josh? He's fifteen."

"Josh. That's a nice name. Hey, how rude of me—I don't even know *your* age." She giggles with a sense of curiosity.

"I'm very old, Jancy!" he responds abruptly.

She nods and says, "Nah. You're far too handsome. Surely you can't be that old. You actually look very young. Can I guess?"

"Sure."

With excitement, she rests her index finger over her lips, staring deeply at his face. Finally she says, "Okay, I got it, Now, as I stare deeply into your sexy hazel eyes, I can see you're younger than what you are telling me. Your skin is so clean; I can tell you don't drink or smoke. Your smile is breathtakingly prominent. Your hair is so thick that I want to run my fingers through it." She halts momentarily, fanning herself with her hand. "You are an incredibly handsome man. Anyway, you should be a lot younger than the age you are describing. In saying this, I believe you'd be thirty-two …?" She gives a cheeky grin, giggles, and then adds, "I'm right, aren't I?" She confidently pumps her fist in the air.

Tom says, "Not quite. I'm turning thirty-six in September."

"Oh, damn! Still, you're not that old, Thomas. So you must've had Josh when you were really young?"

"Yes, we were both very young. Anyway, moving along. We spoke about a several things, till my voice disappeared on me and I could no longer speak. I felt as though the two of them were kind of attacking me, so to speak. I think my emotions were getting the better of me. Josh was fuming, and he wanted answers that I couldn't give him. I knew I was going to say something I was going to regret."

"Two of them?"

"Yes. My ex-wife, Simone, was in the room."

Laney discovers jealousy for the first time in her life. She halts her squinting, trying to understand why she has this sudden sense of jealousy. The first thing to roll off her tongue is, "Did anything happen with Simone?"

He responds, "What do you mean?"

She emotionally continues. "Well, did you guys talk about anything? You know, like trying to start over again, for Josh?"

He sighs. "No, Simone is far too aggravated with me to discuss anything like that. She holds a lot of hatred towards me, yet she still questions my whereabouts or who I am with … I do sense jealousy on her behalf."

Damn! Laney screams loudly within her mind. Then she responds, "Oh, okay. Wow …"

He notes the disheartened state she is in, and he watches as she stares through the windscreen with a look of sorrow. "What are you thinking about?" he asks.

Her attention switches towards Tom. "Mmm …" she responds in a smile. With a look of curiosity, she continues. "My heart is denying me my voice."

"Why's that?"

"Oh, you know, there are some things that one must keep stowed away in one's heart."

"Like what? Speak your mind. I won't judge you …"

"I know you won't judge me. It's your reaction I'm afraid of!" she mumbles, adding gibberish loud enough to get a reaction from Tom.

"What was that?"

She shrugs her shoulders. "Okay, here it goes … Tom, as you may already know, I have …"

His pocket beeps loudly, interrupting Laney. He holds up his index finger at her whilst he checks the message. "Oh, it's Paise …" he says. He opens the message and reads.

"Hey, Tommy. How did it go with Josh? Are you still with him? Please get back to me. Love ya."

Laney notices enough of the message to want to query

it. In the middle of responding to Paisley, she asks, "Hey, Tommy, is Paise a friend of yours?"

He looks to Laney in a confused manner and then replies, "Yes. I've known her for years. Why do you ask?"

"Oh, I just happened to notice the 'love ya' printed at the end of the message."

"Oh, okay." He chuckles at her inquiry. "Well, yes, she always ends her messages that way."

"Right! Are you two, like … really close?"

"Well, yes. We live in the same apartment together."

Devastated at what she has just heard, she shakes her head vigorously, trying to conjure up the right response. "Um, well. Okay! I'm sort of confused."

Sensing the distress within her eyes, he closes his phone and offers her his full attention. "Talk to me, Jancy. Speak your mind. What's confusing you?"

"Well, heck, where do I begin? First and foremost, the obvious question that needs to be uncovered is, what is the story with this Paise? And seriously, what sort of a name is Paise, anyway?" She giggles in jealousy.

He smiles at her inquiry and responds, "Okay, so the story with Paisley …"

She interrupts. "Oh! Paisley! That makes more sense. It's actually quite a beautiful name. Sorry—please continue."

"I've known Paisley for about seven years now," he says. "She was in a very bad place when I met her, but thankfully, she has flourished into something that society now, well, relies on. I'm really proud of whom she has become." He pauses momentarily whilst his mind wanders back in time.

Laney impatiently prompts, "And …?"

He's startled at the loudness of her voice, and he observes her twirling her wrist clockwise, demanding more information. "And what?" he asks in confusion.

"That's it? That's all you are giving me? What about how old she is? And maybe why she is living with you? Why is she saying 'love ya' at the end of her messages? Sorry, but the 'love ya' just isn't sitting well in my tummy. I do feel that you are withholding some vital information."

"She is twenty-eight, and she lives with me because I needed to take care of her and guide her in the right direction. To do this, I needed to keep a close surveillance on her, day and night."

"But why you? Why did you have to look after her?"

"Because I felt I owed a very close friend of mine … He needed me, and she too needed me."

"Right! So how long has she been living with you?" she asks in aggravation.

"Well, the same time as I've known her for … So, six years."

"That's a long bloody time, Tom."

Again his phone interrupts, ringing loudly from inside his pocket. Together they look down to see it's Paise. He looks at Laney and says, "I'm sorry. I really need to take this."

She crosses her arms in anguish, watching him walk away to answer the phone.

"Paise?" he answers.

"Hey, Tommy. Are you okay? I've been so worried about you. I noticed you were trying to type back to me, and then you stopped, so I didn't know what to do. Are you okay? Is Josh okay?"

"Sorry, Paise. I'm with a client right now."

"Oh, okay! Who, Laney?"

Upon hearing the conversation through the loudness of his phone, Laney turns to gaze at him, wondering.

"Yes, I'm with Laney. I'm fine, Paise. I will speak to you when I get home."

Again Laney shakes her head in disbelief.

Paise says, "We've got dinner booked, remember? I told Dad that you were coming too ..."

"Yes, I remember. What time is the reservation?"

"It's 6:30."

"Okay, I should be fine by 6:30."

"But you must come home first to pick me up, yeah?"

"Yes, that's fine. I'll be home in time."

"Okay. Good luck with Laney. Love ya."

When he hangs up the phone, Laney stares diligently at him whilst tapping her foot. With an attentive smirk, he asks, "Janey, what's the matter?"

She furiously retaliates, "What's the matter, he asks. Hmmm, let me think!" She sarcastically asks the ceiling of the vehicle. "Well, where do I start, Tom? How about, how the hell does Paisley know who I am?"

He grins and responds, "You were spoken of last night when I got home."

"Really, now? Well, what gives you the right to speak about my personal business to a complete stranger?"

"Paisley is not a stranger to me ... Janey, we have already been through this. Besides, I didn't speak to Paisley about what we spoke about; she only knows of you, not anything about you. I do not have the right to disclose anything to anyone about anyone's business."

"But why would you even mention me in the first place?"

"Because Paisley is aware of my job, and she actually helps me most of the time. But with you, she knows nothing of you except for your name that society refers to you as."

In disappointment, she vigorously shakes her head. "I confided in you, Tom. I told you things I only ever told Adam. I trusted you as much as I trusted Adam. I loved you. I need to go …" She's aware that she has used the word *love* several times in his presence, but this one here feels different.

In a comforting manner, he says, "Laney, it's not what you are thinking. If it is what I think you are thinking … Listen, I'm here for you, for as long as you need me to be."

"Well, if that's the case, I guess I don't need you anymore."

He bangs his hand on the steering wheel.

Sensing the aggression, she gathers her bag to exit the vehicle. He exits a lot faster and runs around to the passenger side. "Janey, listen to me. You're upset at nothing. Paisley is just a roommate—that is all. I don't and never will speak about what you and I speak about. I care so much about you. I actually haven't stopped thinking about you. I'm strictly here for you. If I don't help you Janey, it'll haunt me for the rest of my life. Do you understand this?" He gazes meticulously at her face and realises the tears are far too constant. With his thumb, he wipes the excess weeping from her cheeks. Then an uncontrollable force of nature pushes him to embrace her.

The sobbing quickly turns into an uncontrollable howl as she rests feebly in his arms. She feels completely safe in his arms; nobody can tease her, bully her, or pester her. *This is what heaven must feel like,* she assures herself.

As their hearts stand face to face, she can feel the love he feels for her. Unfortunately, it's a love that isn't of the *Romeo and Juliet* scenario she was hoping for.

As the embrace comes to a close, she stares at him through her blurry eyes, watching him move into her and attempting to offer her a kiss. Sensing this before it happens, she tilts her head slightly so to feel his lips brush against hers. Tom fearfully pulls his head away, but Laney captures it. She stands vulnerable with her eyes closed and lips pouted. Time ceases for her. The only visible things to her are the park, the tree, herself and Tom, and the bright sun that shines upon them.

The park is empty; the world is theirs. Society and all it carries with it has been abolished, just from this one inadvertent kiss. Noticing her in her dream state, he smiles and chooses to leave her be.

They remain deeply embraced, sitting by the enormous green tree, staring up at the bright blue sky. Tom suddenly turns to look at her and says, "Paise, wake up."

Startled, she awakens and says, "Shit. Did you just call me Paise?"

"What? No! No way! I was screaming, *Janey, wake up.* You were away in another world."

"I can't do this anymore, Tom! I just can't do it …"

"What the hell? What just happened? Janey, wait." In an agitated state, he grabs her wrist before she is able to walk off.

"What, Tom?" she responds in frustration.

"What is wrong? I am here to help you, remember?"

"Okay, you want to help me? Then please just let me go.

I love you, Tom! I love you in the tree-engraving way. I'm so sorry." She attempts to walk away again.

He grabs hold of her and says, "Janey, wait …"

She shrugs off his arm and says, "No. I'm deeply sorry that my heart has fallen for you, Tom. I know yours doesn't feel the same way. The only way I am able to deal with this is to let you go. So please just let *me* go."

He rebuts, "Janey, you are sixteen. I am thirty-six. You have a very long life ahead of you. You love me because I understand you, I help you, and I listen to you. Your heart is miscommunicating with your mind. You are far too young to love someone as old as me."

"Don't you dare speak for me, let alone for my heart!?" She points to her chest. "This is *my* heart. I control this heart, not you." She tries to catch her breath. "My heart is always right, Tom. You may not believe it, but I do. Adam told me I must always follow my heart, and I make sure I do. You know what? Can you please just go away? Please, Tommy. Please just go away." In an uncontrollable bawl, she looks to the concrete floor, realising that the only person who could ever hold her as tight as she wants him to is no longer worthy of holding her at all.

Unexpectedly, a voice from in the distance alerts them to its presence. "Hey, is there some sort of a problem here, mate?"

Their attention switches towards the large red home to notice a rather large man standing by the garage door.

Not wanting to cause a scene, Laney hurriedly says, "Sorry, mister. It's fine. This is my uncle, and we were just talking. Thank you for your concern, though." She turns back to Tom. "I'm fine. I'll walk home from here. Thank you for everything."

In annoyance, he knows he must not push the matter, so he stands helpless, watching her walk away.

CHAPTER 26

Inside at the Right Time

"Mum, I'm still at Ben's, okay?"

"I was wondering when you were going to call. You've been there for a while!"

While peeking through the bedroom window, Ben spots the commotion outside. He interrupts Josh. "Dude, my dad is telling some guy off in the street."

Josh ignores him and keeps conversing with his mother. "Yeah, I'll be leaving soon, Mum. Are you still gonna pick me up?"

"Um, you never mentioned that. I don't even know where he lives, honey."

"Are you serious? That big, bloody red house?" He chuckles.

"Oh, yes. Well, what time do you want me to pick you up?"

Abruptly changing his mind, Josh says, "Nah, don't worry about it. I'll walk home. At least it'll give me time to think."

"Oh, okay, honey. Just don't leave too late."

"I'm actually gonna leave real soon, so don't stress. Okay, I'm going." Upon disconnecting the call, he walks to the window where Ben is staring. He notices a female who appears worthy of his attention. "Benny, who's that bird walking?" he asks, pointing at the girl.

"Oh, I don't know her, man. I see her walking down this street all the time, though. I think she's cute."

"She looks it from here. Anyway, Mum's not picking me up, so I'd better leave now if I'm gonna make it home by dinner."

CHAPTER 27

Take the Long Way Home

Lacey is dealing with an emotional sense of betrayal. She walks down the street, staring at the concrete foot path and going over her thoughts. *Adam, is it true? Did my heart not communicate accurately with my mind? I know what I feel. I know it's true love that I feel for him, and not in the friendly way. I mean, you saw it yourself. Did he not love me in the same way? Did I misinterpret his emotional state towards me? How did I not see that his love was of a friendly nature? I misread that completely ... But I felt it! I read it in his beautiful eyes, his smirks, his voice. I'm sorry, but I refuse to believe that his feelings aren't equal to mine. I mean, you know what special senses I have, Adam. I know for a fact that he does love me. I know he does ...*

What am I to do now? I will not be able to let him go, even if I try. It'll eat at me, consume me in a way where I won't want to live anymore. Adam, what do I do? I need you now ... I need my Tommy.

Her train of thought diminishes upon hearing footsteps and deep breathing rapidly approaching her. She turns to spot a boy who stands around 168 centimetres tall with dark hair that's left messy in style but is suitable for his face. His hazel eyes resemble a certain person she knows, but she can't quite pick it. She notices how strikingly handsome he is.

"Can I help you?" she asks antagonistically.

"Um," he responds awkwardly. Then with a mischievous smile, he watches her giggle with a sense of concealment.

"Do I know you?" she asks, somehow captivated by his grin.

"No, I can't say you do. But I'm glad I know you now."

She begins chuckling at his statement and then says, "But you don't know me yet! I haven't even announced my name to you."

He shakes his head and responds, "That is completely fine! You see, your pretty features are more than enough, for me to tell myself that I will never forget this beautiful girl's face."

At a loss of words, she stands helpless. Then manages to retort, "Well, that's kinda straightforward, don't you think?"

He sighs. "Life is far too short to waste time on wondering when you have the right of knowing."

"I can definitely relate to that." While fanning herself with her hands, suddenly she finds herself feeling flustered from the charms of this familiar-looking, handsome boy.

He confidently holds his hand out to her and says, "Hi. My parents named me Josh."

She giggles flirtatiously, accepts his hand, and replies, "Hi, Josh. Society has named me Laney."

"Well, I say fuck society. What have your parents named you?"

With a conspicuous smile, she responds, "I'm not quite sure if I'm ready to give up the name my parents labelled me with."

"Really?" he asks disappointingly. "I just shared mine ..."

"Yeah, I'm not ready. Sorry."

"That's fine! I will wait till you're ready, then. Hey, did I mention how pretty you are, Laney?"

She laughs at his inhibition. "Why, thank you, Josh!" Upon hearing herself speak the name Josh, it instantly clicks. She pauses with her eyes wide open in surprise, recalling his smile, his hazel eyes, the vague similarity, and the name. She then looks up to the sky, and in her mind she says, *Adam, was this you?*

Upon observing her meditative state, he snaps his fingers at her and says, "Hello, Laney? Are you still with me?"

She shakes her head, snapping herself out of it. "I'm so sorry, Josh." After giggling with humiliation, she adds, "My mind suddenly went astray due to the fact that I know you. I can't explain how I know you, but I just do. The reason why I was looking up to the sky was because I was talking to my cousin, who looks down on me all the time and answers a lot of my questions."

He points to the heavens. "Your cousin? Up there?" She nods in acknowledgement. "I wish I had someone up there that would look down on me."

"Well, you do. Everybody does. Everybody has the universe to ask for help, I know I do, but I still choose to speak with my cousin."

"So who is this cousin?"

"His name is Adam. He passed away years ago... I don't want to get into it right now—sorry."

"No, don't be sorry. Maybe one day in the very near future, you can tell me about Adam. Maybe over a coffee?"

"Shit, we'll need more than a coffee—we'll need a lifetime."

Whilst she giggles, he says, "Hopefully a lifetime is what we'll have, then." He blushes upon announcing it but feels content within himself by being able to deliver it the way he did.

"Wow!" she says.

"Wow?"

"Yeah, wow." She starts laughing hysterically.

"Was that a little too straightforward for you, Laney?"

"No, no way. I am actually amazed at how alike you are …" She pauses abruptly, holding her hand to her mouth.

"Whoa—you almost let that spill out of that pretty little mouth of yours. Tell me, Laney, who shares the same likeness as I?"

"Oh." Upon realising she has made a terrible mistake, she continues, "Oh, no one special … Just somebody I know. A real down-to-earth, straight-to-the-point person. The resemblance between the two of you is unbelievable."

"It's not Adam, is it?" he asks curiously.

"God, no. Adam was completely opposite you …"

"Oh, okay! Well, is he better looking than me?" He holds a solid grin with a sense of jealousy, curious about this person.

"Well, I did state how the resemblance was amazing. So yes, the both of you are very good looking. Wait, did I just say that out aloud? Jesus. Man, stop asking me these questions, Josh!"

He laughs at her quirkiness and notices her looking ahead of her. "Hey, you live far? Would you like some company on your journey home?"

She contemplates the offer. After noticing Josh gawking at her, she says, "Josh, you need to give me a couple minutes for this offer to sink in. I need to decide on the pros and cons. Will you allow me the two minutes?"

Smiling at her honesty, he replies, "Take three if you need to. Hell, I'll wait an eternity for you. But on one condition. Would you allow for me to gaze upon that beautiful face whilst you decide?"

She smiles in a flirtatious manner and says, "Sure. Gaze to your heart's content."

To shorten the length of her thought process, she deletes one of the major thoughts: any sort of a rape scene occurring on this trip home. She firmly believes that he is a genuinely nice boy, especially given he's the son of her new friend Tom. *I doubt he'll be that type of person. I actually think he'll be of nice company, and I know he'll make me laugh. I need some humour after what just happened with Tom. My question to myself is, will he try something on me? Or will he be a gentleman and just walk me home? He is cute, though …* When the thought process ends, she perceives the gaze he holds over her. She smiles as he points to his invisible timepiece, which is invisibly wrapped around his wrist.

He silently mouths, "It's been four minutes. You told me three."

From that one moment, she bursts out laughing, holding her stomach from the pain of severe laughter. After she gets her breath back, she responds, "Okay, okay. Walk me home already."

CHAPTER 28

Dinner Got Cancelled

Upon hearing the garage door open up from inside the kitchen, Paisley runs towards the door to leap onto Tom for a much-needed embrace. Pecking endless amounts of kisses over his cheek, she says, "Oh, God, Tommy. Are you okay? I've been so worried since I left you at Josh's home." She moves into him, applying more kisses over his cheeks.

He smiles in admiration as he gazes at her pretty face. "I'm fine, Paise! I just want to get ready for tonight."

Unconvinced, she rebuts, "But you don't *seem* fine, Tommy! You look sad."

He's aware that she knows him so well. He can't hide his emotions from her. "It didn't go so well with Laney earlier. I made her upset."

She grabs hold of his hand and walks him into the house. "Oh, no," she says, offering him a seat over the sofa. "Just sit here! I'll make you a coffee, and then we'll talk about it."

"I thought we were going to dinner?" he says.

With a smirk, she replies, "Oh, no. It got cancelled. I'm making dinner tonight. Unless you want to get takeout?"

"Okay, what are you making?"

She smiles. "Your favourite, of course: steak with mushroom sauce and veggies."

He nods appreciatively and watches her place the freshly brewed coffee on a little table that displays a photo of her, Tom, and an unidentifiable man. He's seated tranquilly whilst they enjoy their coffee.

Paisley has a notion and says, "Hey, you wanna watch a film after dinner?"

He smiles and gazes at the delightfulness she conveys. Noticing his smile, she slaps his thigh, holds her hand there, and then says, "What are you smirking at, Tommy? Huh?" She tickles his leg.

"I'm smiling at how wonderful you are, Paise. You're so good to me."

Instantly she expresses a smile of timidity. "That's cos I love ya, Tommy boy."

They're seated in silence, and finally their eyes have the opportunity to meet. She sensuously bites her bottom lip and notices Tom gazing at her in surprise. She subtly uses his gaze as an invitation to slowly move in closer towards him, hoping he doesn't reject her. He hasn't moved an inch, so she welcomingly plants her lips delicately over his. Somewhat startled by her tenacity, he slowly tries moving back as she continuously pushes forward. With not much room to spare, he unexpectedly finds the armrest blocking his escape plan. By this period, her lips have touched his for the second time. His mind yearns for her lips as much as she does, but blocking the passion he yearns for are images of Lancy. The tempting sensation of her soft, moist lips is not helping him to pull out of this. She forcefully blankets his lips with her mouth sucking them as she detaches. He reluctantly senses an instant pleasure towards Paisley's tenacity, but the images keep flooding the space in his head.

Is this wrong of me, to have my feelings for Laney reach a point where my heart has chosen? I have Paisley—whom I shouldn't be doing this with anyway, but I so badly want to ... I'm in an emotional state where I want love from someone, but this love I want is from Laney, not just from anyone ... But she is sixteen! I can't have these feelings for her. What am I saying?

Her hand has made its way to his crotch, feeling his erection through his jeans. She gently squeezes the shaft as Tom keeps trying to escape deeper into the sofa. From the extent of his erection, it is proof enough that he wants this as much as Paisley. Yet he finds himself trying to fight off the emotions he feels for Laney. Visions of her young, beautiful face—the same face that told him she loves him—overpowers all other thoughts.

With a sudden break in the kiss, he quickly mumbles, "Paise, we can't do this."

She ignores him and starts to become more aggressive in her kissing. Unwittingly, her tongue circles his entire mouth in search of a spot to rest. Through the talents of multitasking, she manages to unzip his jeans. The difficult task that lies ahead of her is how she will remove his pants.

Her hand has managed to find a new home, entering through the zip of his jeans, against his underwear. Through the barricade of the underwear, she continues massaging his penis through the discomfort of the zip, which makes indenting marks against her skin. He sits idle and vulnerable, offering no sense of help at all towards this attempted rape.

The ache in his heart speaks the name of another, a person who, his mind insists, is far too young for him. His attention re focuses on the beauty seated before him.

He finally gives in, allowing Paisley full access to whatever she chooses to do. She finds her way through the underwear to grasp hold of his penis. An instant moan comes from his mouth upon the initial touch from her soft fingers. His hands remain pressed hard against the pillow of the sofa, trying his hardest to fight off this urge. But in the midst of his penis being stroked so delicately, her mouth seeks other regions of his body, coating her wet saliva over his bare skin.

With her other hand, she lifts up his top, trying to get Tom to help her remove it. In a frustrating manner, he gives in, removing it for her. She smiles at his bare chest, knowing she has full access to taste all she wants to. In the midst of leaving her markings over his chest, she continues pleasuring him by giving his stiff penis proficient strokes.

CHAPTER 29

The Narrator

*S*orry, readers. Unfortunately, we need to bypass some of this scene due to Laney's scene being far more important. I am aware that this scene with Paisley and Tom is so enticing, but Laney's thoughts are far more significant at this stage.

I'm home now, and he hasn't tried anything on me. What a gentleman he truly is. But why do I find myself still thinking about Tom? I wonder what he is doing. I feel bad for speaking to him the way I did. But I do feel sorry for Josh, because I'm not even giving him my full attention. How can I, when all I have is Tom's beautiful face, his beautiful words, his beautiful heart embedded in all of me?

Why has Josh miraculously entered into my life? Is it the universe's way of saying I can't have Tom? If this is why Josh is here, I am not impressed. I mean, he's cute and all, and he looks like Tom and acts like Tom. But unfortunately, he isn't my Tom-Tom. Actually, I think I need to message Tom. I'll say my thank-you and goodbye to Josh, and then I'll text Tom right away.

Before she is able to speak a word to Josh, he says, "Hey, Laney, do you think I can have your number? You know, just in case I need someone to talk to while I walk home?"

She giggles at his request and stops to think.

Interesting! Do I give the son of the man I love my private phone number? Is this the right thing to do? Adam?

He interrupts her thoughts. "So how did it go? What did your mind decide on?"

"How do you mean?"

"Well, you were having a conversation in your head again, and I am curious as to how it went in regards to giving me your number. Was there a response of any sort?"

She laughs and offers him the benefit of the doubt. "Okay, you ready? My number is 0426965321! If you can't remember that, it's your loss. Which means you weren't paying attention, which also means you're not really interested in me. Now, if you'll excuse me, I need to send a text to someone." In a teasing fashion, she slowly walks away. Then after several meters, she turns her head to spot him still typing. Once his eyes make contact with hers, she gives a subtle wave at him.

CHAPTER 30

Back to Paisley and Tom

After finally winning the battle in removing his pants, Paise stands on the pants, forcing them down to his ankles. She fiddles with the underwear scarcely covering his privates, exposing the head of his penis. She removes her top, exposing her sexy black bra.

She uses both hands to unbutton her jeans and effortlessly slide them down to the floor. While he watches the swift movements of her pants dropping, his penis erects a little bit more, and he gazes at her black G-string. This one performance was more than enough for him to finally choose to operate his hands at his advantage.

He rests his warm hands around her waist to hold her in position. Fighting the hold, she kisses him violently, as though to punish him for taking so long to give in to her. He accepts the violence and kisses her back. With her right hand, she exposes the rest of his penis from his underwear to fiddle around with it, reacquainting herself with it. She skilfully massages the head of his penis by rubbing her thumb against the raw head. While she is busy tantalising him, his hands slide down her waist to her bare bottom, squeezing her soft, smooth cheeks. Gritting his teeth, he tightly grasps them, spreading them apart and allowing the G-string to slide into her drenched lower regions. She moans from the aggression of the squeeze, and then with her spare hand, she unlatches her bra waiting, on Tom to remove it for her.

Upon noticing the slackening of her bra, his hands unlatch the grasp on her behind, moving up to her shoulders to unlatch the strings. He watches the bra sassily slide off, finally exposing her firm, perky breasts. Her little nipples are fully erect from desire and the coldness of the air. Upon gazing down at them, timidly she holds a smile whilst biting her lower lip.

He can't help but gaze deeply at them, amazed at what he is witnessing. He wants to marvel at her perfection as much as he can before he covers them with the palms of his warm hands. In excitement, he finally places both hands gently over each breast, softly squeezing them. A distant vibrating sound interrupts the frolicking he is enduring. He flicks his head to the side, trying to have a clearer listen of where the sound comes from.

He doesn't hear it again, so he resumes the caressing of her breasts, admiring their plumpness. His teeth clench once again. He dampens his lips and then places his mouth around the nipple of her right breast. She moans, rolling her head back in ecstasy. His tongue licks the nipple, circling it and applying an unexpected tickling sensation. Sharing in the fun, he moves towards her left breast, applying the same technique far more vigorously.

She feels an overwhelming frenzy and can't handle it any longer. She raises herself to hover over him and then latches the base of the G-string with her finger, offering room to rub the head of his penis against her saturated vagina. Mischievously, she grinds her wet mound over the exposed head of his penis, awaiting an effortless insertion.

Both parties moan in ecstasy as the full length of his penis penetrates deeply inside of her. With each grind she administers against him, she whines from the orgasmic sensation she endures. His eyes entertain themselves as she sensually moves her sexy body up and down. In a combination of everything, his ejaculation rapidly approaches. With her eyes sealed shut, she vigorously grinds harder, desiring more depth. As her movements become swifter, the pressure she applies against him hurriedly turns her moans into much louder groans.

Through the intensity of her groans, he manages to detect another distant vibrating sound. Glancing behind him, he says to Paisley, "Can you hear that?"

She puts her finger over his lips and says, "Shh!"

Obeying her demand, he grips her bare bottom, firmly squeezing her cheeks. While gritting his teeth once again, he stretches her cheeks apart, allowing for an extra millimetre of insertion. Listening to the loud groans echoing from her, he yearns for a faster, more aggressive climax. In doing so, he raises his pelvis in sync to her movements. This one movement denies him the patience he once had to hold off on his climax. Having lost all sense of control, he looks to her. "Paise, I can't hold it anymore."

She grinds harder and moans, "Oh, oh, oh! Just release it inside me!"

Disregarding the consequential place of ejaculation, he

willingly releases his sperm inside her as she demands. Upon the explosive release, he raises his torso, fighting the shivering feeling she is currently enduring. She pressures the weight of her body down onto his so he can release his sperm deep inside of her. Feeling the ejaculation circulate within her, she implodes severely, screaming in her loudest voice. Her body quivers in unison with her orgasm. Out of puff, she rests her torso on his trying, her absolute hardest to keep breathing.

"Oh, my god!" she says pleasantly.

Holding this long-awaited embrace, she kisses at his neck in a pecking fashion, tickling him in the process. He giggles, trying to force her away. Then together they hear the resonance of a vibrating sound from in the distance.

CHAPTER 31

So Many Messages

At 6:56 p.m., Tom opens his phone to a page filled with text messages. He comprehends why he was hearing the sound of vibrations. "Shit!" he says, realising the messages are all from Laney. Without wasting any time, he swipes the messages to read them.

The first message came in at 6:02 p.m. and read, "Hi, Tom-Tom. Listen, I'm so sorry about earlier today. I got caught up in the moment, and after seeing the messages from Paisley (beautiful name, by the way), I freaked. Please message me back."

At 6:12 p.m. she wrote, "Tom-Tom, I hope you're not ignoring me. I told you I'm sorry. I'll be good now, I promise ..."

At 6:22 p.m.: "Okay, Tommy, you're freaking me out now. I comprehend the situation with Paisley. I'm fine about it. I know the two of you are just close friends. I over-reacted. Please reply."

At 6:30 p.m.: "Can't you just reply to me, please? I'm crying, Tom ..."

Then at 6:43 p.m. she wrote, "I don't know what else

to do. I've tried talking to Adam, but he isn't giving me any signs. There's only one thing left to do …"

Instinctively, he exits the message to dial her. The phone rings out without a response. He dials out again. After another session of unresponsive rings, he says, "Shit. I've gotta call Brandon." He realises the time—Brandon has already left the office.

"Paise?" he screams. He hears the flow of water from within the bathroom and heads towards her.

She's startled by the rapid intrusion and says, "Tommy, what's wrong?"

"Paise, I need to get Lancy's address somehow."

She exits the shower unclothed. "Okay, baby. Give me a sec." She swiftly wraps a towel around herself. "Dad's left the office, but I should be able to access it from my computer. I have access to everyone's details." Already by her computer, she searches the clients and asks, "Is Lancy okay? You seem terrified …"

"I don't think she is okay, Paise. I must go to her now, before she does something bad—if she hasn't already."

Seconds later, she shares the link to his phone and accepts a simple kiss on her forehead as a thank-you.

CHAPTER 32

A Very Long Drive

What the hell am I gonna do if Janey has caused harm to herself? This was not supposed to happen. Definitely not to Janey ...

"Come on. Get out of the way, you useless driver!" he screams from inside his vehicle, unaware of his speed.

This is it. This is going to be the death of me. I won't come out of this ... Please be alive, Janey!

Three minutes away. Come on—I'm almost there.

"Three minutes, three minutes, three minutes," he mutters to himself, unaware that his attention for the road has completely disappeared. But somebody, a higher being, is watching over him tonight; he has cheated death several times on this, the longest journey he has ever encountered.

CHAPTER 33

Laney's Home

As Tom pulls up to the home, he spots no vehicles in the driveway, nor a garage where a car could be resting. He parks the car on the street across the road, casually exits his vehicle, and walks to the front of the house as discreetly as possible. Having already decided in his head how to go about this, he chooses to dial her again. It rings through again. He stands at the front door, takes several deep breaths, and then bangs his fist three times on the door.

After a minute or two of impatiently waiting, he applies three more thuds against the door. Having no such luck, he notices a crack in the curtain that he can peek through, observing some of the home's inside. The house seems to be sealed up for the night.

Whilst peering through the window, he dials out to her again. Upon hearing the ringing tone from his own phone, he notices flashing lights in the distant darkness of the house. He waits till it rings out to notice the flashing lights have stopped when he hangs up.

The lack of a response can only mean that she left the phone at home and went out, or she can't hear it ringing because she is doing something. The latter of the explanations leads to something he refuses to disclose to the universe.

Having discovered he has no other alternative, he paces back to the door, thumping as loudly as he can in hope for a response. He tries the handle, and then he checks the street behind him. Slowly, he turns the handle all the way to surprisingly push the door open. His mind wonders why the door was left unlocked. He then has one last glance at the street behind him before he casually walks into the home.

To his left, he spots a vacant bedroom with an open door. To the right of him, he distinguishes a lounge area through the darkness of the home. After closing the door behind him, he calls out, "Janey, are you here?" After no response, he thinks swiftly, recalling the flashing lights he witnessed seconds ago. With his phone plastered to his palm, he dials out to her again, hearing the resonance of the vibration from in another room. Through the darkened lounge area, he notices the flashing lights from what looks to be in the kitchen area. He heads towards it and realises the phone was left upside down on the kitchen table. He gathers it up and flips it around, observing the words "My love Tom-Tom calling."

He screams out, "Janey!" While holding her phone in his hand, he switches on the kitchen light. The room lights up, and on the dinner table is a note sitting beside her phone. He reads it.

Mum,

    I'm truly sorry about the dirty dishes. Unfortunately, I didn't get a chance to do them. I feel really sad today—probably the saddest I've ever felt.

By the time you read this, I'm sure I will have already left to meet Adam. I love you, Mum. I have always loved you, and I know that everything you did was for me. I just get angry, because all I want is to spend time with you, but life always gets in the way.

Anyway, I met a man yesterday whom I knew I was going to meet. This man is the most beautiful, kind-hearted man I've ever met. He helped me, changed my way of thinking, and made me understand that I do have a purpose in life.

I was meaning to sit with you, to discuss what we will be able to do to see each other more often, but I never got around to actually sitting down with you.

Anyway, this man's name is Tom. I'm in love with him. I know it may sound far-fetched, but I do feel it in my heart. I made a very bad decision today: I told him to go away when I shouldn't have, and now he hates me.

Mum, Adam spoke to me at 6:45 p.m. He told me this life isn't the one for me. My next life is one where I'll be a lot happier, and therefore Adam is waiting for me to come to him. I'll be gone by the time you get home. Please tell Tom that I loved him with all my heart. I will miss him, and I'll miss you. Know that I'll always look down on the both of you, and I will protect you both.

Love always and forever,

Laney

A tear of sorrow drops to the letter, smudging an area. He desperately searches the room in search of a clock and finds one: 7:13 p.m. His mind displays images of Laney being hung from the ceiling. Petrified at the thought, he runs about the home to spot a door at the end of the hall, with a ray of light beaming through the crack at the bottom.

Sprinting down the darkened hallway of the home, he turns the handle of the door, only to discover Laney lying afloat in the water of the bath. Her eyes are darkened, her skin is pale, and he immediately fears the worst.

With haste, he places his hands under her lifeless body, pulling her out of the cold water and carrying her into the bedroom beside the bathroom. Lying her feeble body over the bed, he hovers over her, places his mouth over hers, and then presses his palms to her chest, applying his form of resuscitation. He does this for over thirty seconds, until he stops to punch the bed.

"Janey, you are not dying on me. Not today!" he screams loudly whilst pounding her chest. After the tenth press on her chest, he felt her fingers brush against his leg. As he looked to her hand, he finds it's formed into a fist. In hope, he vigorously keeps at her chest and mouth till he feels her chest expand against his hands. Then watches a cup of water cough out of her mouth.

CHAPTER 34

She's Alive

Through the cough, the water dribbles down the side of her cheeks. Then suddenly the top half of her body raises off the bed. She coughs loudly, her eyes open and displaying the deep redness within them. His initial reaction is to hurriedly embrace her, assuring her that he will never let her go.

Completely unaware of what happened, her arms rest flaccid over the bed. Upon realising it is Tom, she feebly raises her arms to return the embrace. She smiles at the sight of him and then croaks, "Tom-Tom, you saved me!"

He releases the embrace to gaze into her bloodshot eyes.

Still croaky, she adds, "I knew you'd come for me, you know. That's why I left the door unlocked." Remorsefully, he moves into her again, embracing her as tightly as he can. His flowing tears blend with the excess bathwater that hasn't yet evaporated from her shivering body.

"Tom, you're squeezing me too tightly."

He still holds the remorseful embrace.

"I'm freezing." The shiver within her voice is an understanding for him to hurriedly rest her frail body on the bed.

Trying to keep her as warm as he can, he wraps her body

in the blanket and then picks her up to cradle her in his lap as he would a baby.

"This is nice. You wrapped me up like a cocoon."

His vocal chords have vanished due to the trepidation he felt only minutes ago. He knows that she should be taken to the hospital right now, but he is also aware that they may place her in a mental institution. His heart knows he must deal with this alone—and deal with this now. Yet that daunting suicide note appears over and over in his head. His sorrowful tears keep pouring out from under his eyes. and he's incapable of holding back the true feelings he holds for her.

"Tom, say something ..." She coughs again. He clenches his teeth together in anger, and squeezes her tightly. "Tom-Tom? I should be the one crying. You just saw all my privates!"

With a slight shake of the head, he manages to reveal a smile at her inquest. Then he says, "Janey, you scared the living shit out of me. Do you have any idea how I just felt minutes ago? If I lost you, I would've taken my own life too. Do you not realise this?"

"Oh, you should've just left me and followed through. We could've been together forever."

He shakes his head, adding, "It doesn't work that way, Janey. How do you know we would've been together?"

With her arms trapped in the blanket, she blows shots of air towards her eyes, trying to relieve an itch. Upon noticing her struggle, he releases the blanket to free her arm. Finally she rebuts, "You're wrong, Tom. I spoke to Adam, and he told me that we will be together in heaven."

"How did you speak to Adam?"

"Well, remember how I explained it's practically

impossible to kill yourself? Guess what? Adam helped me, and that's how I was able to do it."

Bewildered, he responds, "So my reviving you—what has that caused?"

"Nothing! I knew you would save me. I asked Adam about it, and he just smiled at me. That's when I knew you would come to my rescue. I was still needed on this earth—he told me."

"But that doesn't make any sense. You told me he helped you to commit suicide and then let you come back. If he helped you, why would he let you come back?"

"Well, I told Adam that if you came to my rescue, I wanted to go back to be with you." She pauses.

He impatiently says, "And …?"

"And I should've been dead, already. Tom, cos you came way too late. But when they saw how hard you were trying, they decided to let me come back. But they had conditions …"

"Conditions?" he repeats.

"Yeah. I need to be 100 per cent truthful about the feelings that I have for you. But I'm sure you are already aware of them."

CHAPTER 35

Laney's True Feelings

$\mathcal{L}$aney shifts about whilst resting in Tom's arms, and she finally adjusts to a comfortable position. Noticing her discomfort, he says, "I'll step out of the room so you can put on something." He sets her on the bed.

She frees an arm to soften the landing and says, "No, Tom. Please, I want you to hold me in your arms. I want to feel safe."

He happily continues holding her. Comprehending the dampness of her hair, he adds, "I think you should dry off and then cover yourself with clothing. You are shivering, Janey."

She gives a sensual kiss to her index finger and places it against his lips. "Its fine, my gentleman." She smiles and continues. "Just hold me. That is all I'll ever want or need." In the comfort of his warm embrace, she says, "Okay, I think I am ready to reveal my true feelings. How do I begin? How do I say this? I'm sure you are completely aware of this already, Tom, but here it goes ... Tom, I am madly in love with you, and definitely not in a friendly way. My heart has chosen the *Romeo and Juliet* way. I would actually die for you. Do you realise this? I know you may think I'm going crazy, and that my feelings are this way because you are so nice to me and have helped me. This is definitely not the case. You see, I can assure you right now that my feelings are completely real. I had at one stage thought that I was in love with Jacob. Remember when I told you about him?" He nods in acknowledgement. "Yeah well, I thought that was love. That wasn't love, Tom. I had a crush on a boy who was really good looking. That was all. True love? True love is you and me. I've only known you for two days, and I fell for you in that instant. Do you understand? It was actually love at first sight. I felt it in my mind, my body, and most important my heart. You made me feel things in my body that I have never felt before—sexual things. I was actually wet down there." She giggles while blushing.

"I know I'm only sixteen, and I'm totally aware of your age. Believe me, I have thought long and hard about it. But I do know what I want. If you left me now, Tom, and I somehow found it in my heart to not leave this earth the way I tried to already, I can tell you now that I will never find a love like yours again. You're my love at first sight. I will never be able to move on, or be with anyone else. Look, I'm not sure exactly how you feel towards me, but I can somewhat feel your true feelings. When we embrace, I feel your heart speak to mine. Did you know that our hearts communicate more than us? The little suckers."

He chuckles at her, but she scolds him. "I'm not playing, Tom-Tom. If you could hear them like I do, you'd know they are both little chatterboxes, yapping away about anything and everything. But you know what? They have found each other, and they discovered that they don't want to be apart."

She places her arms around him and politely demands, "Can you please say something?"

His response is to pull away from her grasp and straighten her torso whilst she remains seated on his lap, so he has the freedom to fall back onto the bed.

She relentlessly rotates her body to face him. With this sudden change of seating, he unquestionably senses the discomfort within his heart. The fact that she is naked under that blanket makes matters a lot worse. The loosened blanket opens slightly to expose her breasts. He quickly covers his eyes and then feels Laney bend her torso to whisper into his ear.

"Tom, talk to me, please …"

He responds, "Janey, you are too young for me. This is wrong for you to have these feelings. I am far too old to have any sort of feelings …"

Unexpectedly, the vibration from his phone alerts the both of them. Laney demands, "Please just leave it, Tom. Leave it!" She screams, tears falling from her eyes. He knows he can't leave it, and so he fiddles around in his pocket to notice a new message from Paisley.

"You've gotta be kidding me. Tom, can you please just leave it?"

He reads the message: "Hey, Tom. How did you go with Laney? Hurry home, please. I miss you." He accesses the keyboard to reply.

Janey says, "You're not listening to me! I'm asking for you to leave it." He continues his reply. "You happily chose to ignore my messages!"

He rebuts, "I didn't ignore your messages, Janey. I was busy doing … something."

"Doing what, Tom? Doing Paisley?"

"Janey, that's enough! My phone happened to be on silent, so I didn't hear it beep. Now, if I don't message her back right away, she is going to call me." He continues with the message.

In agitation, Janey hops off his lap to lay foetal on the bed. She then covers her face with the blanket that Tom has draped over her.

"Janey, it's cold. I want you to put something on, please …"

"No!" she screams. She uncovers her face from the blanket, and adds, "What's bloody wrong with you, Tom? Are you upset at me or something? You're not yourself, and don't for one second think that I don't see it. Why can't you just talk to me?" Again she covers her face.

Tom places his hand over her hip to control her shivering body. He then moves his hand to rub her back through the blanket draped over her. "Janey, you really need to get some rest."

"Well, can you stay with me tonight? I mean, what if I feel the same way again?"

He shakes his head. "Janey, I can't stay here! For starters, your mum will be home soon."

"No! She is doing the late shift tonight. She left thirty minutes before you got here, and she won't be home until six in the morning."

"Janey, I'm sorry. I can't stay here—I just can't! I really want to, but I mustn't."

"What is your heart telling you to do, Tom?"

Before delivering his response, he ponders to find that

his heart wants him to stay. But his second voice—the voice that at times takes command and responds before his heart— orders him to go home. What's baffled him is that the second in command usually just speaks for Tom and doesn't care when his heart loses out. But the hesitation involved in this decision has left him stunned in bewilderment.

"Does it really take you this long to communicate with your heart, Tom? If that's the case, I feel for you. My heart notifies me in an instant." He's at a loss of words and fails to respond. "That's okay! I get it, Tom. I understand. Refusing to listen to your heart is the obvious decision you've made." She tosses off the blanket off to seat her naked body down directly beside him. "Its fine, Tom. I won't attempt to kill myself again. I promise. I'm far too tired, anyway. And just for the record, I wasn't planning to have sex with you. All I wanted was for you to hold me in your arms, just so I could feel safe and maybe have that sense of relief, where I could finally catch up on the sleep that I have missed out on for over six years."

Showing no sign of discomfiture towards him, she stands up and seats her nude body over a chair covered in several sorts of attire. She scrounges through every piece, trying to find a suitable option. As she does so, he stares at her perfect, untainted derrière. Then he focuses his eyes on the floor, trying to fight off the erection coming from the cover of his jeans.

Knowing she is still standing unclothed, his eyes move towards her figure again before his mind has a chance to stop it.

She's aware of having her perfect figure on display, and she uses time to find something to cover herself. His eyes remain gazing at every part of her body that is visible from his angle.

Then unexpectedly, he has a sudden change of heart. He

stands and says, "Janey, enough. I cannot do this. We cannot do this!"

She turns around, knowing that his eyes have been vigorously admiring her. Then she walks towards him and says, "Tom, please. I'll get dressed. Please just stay with me." In a platonic manner, she presses her naked body against his, making him aware that she is looking for somebody to hold her. "Tom, please hold me."

Upon hearing her sulking, he finally realises he can't allow for her to endure any more suffering; it is breaking his heart. He throws his arms around her, disregarding any sexual thoughts he may have left inside him.

The embrace is the kind Laney is longing for, pleading for. As the embrace transpires, Laney feels the warmth, the comfort, the innocence all in the one occurrence. She tightly holds onto the love of her life.

Five minutes pass, and finally the embrace comes to an end. The attire she was searching for is never found. She chooses the foetal position she endured only minutes ago, remaining unprotected. Tom covers her with the blanket and then lays beside her.

There is a silence of pure bliss, a calm where both hearts can finally communicate amongst each other, a peace where both souls have united to become one. At the thought of their hearts conversing, she begins to giggle.

The pace of her breath has drastically reduced. She feels safe, and the drowsiness quickly approaches. The warmth of his body against hers allows her to finally cave in and close her eyes.

Five minutes since she made her last movement, he

realises she is fast asleep. While his arm is around her, his heart demands for him to remain where he is. He knows that if she wakes up to not find him there, her reaction may lead to desperate measures.

Disrupting his dubious mind are visions of Paisley calling his phone to disturb Lancy's sleep. He knows he must call her to explain the predicament he is in. This will take a phone call because a simple message won't cut it. Lancy remains completely motionless, and her breaths have become steady.

After fiddling with his jeans pocket, he grasps his phone to find a message from Paisley. "Baby, is everything okay? Please message me back." He received that message at 9:27 p.m., and it is now 9:49 p.m.

Shit! I've gotta ring her straight away. Realising he has a mission ahead of him, he knows he must exit the bed without waking Lancy. He delicately removes the blanket to free his legs in preparation for evacuating the bed. He smoothly slides out of the bed undetected.

Upon exiting the bedroom, he heads back to the kitchen, where he found the suicide note Lancy had written. He grabs it from the table and places it in his back pocket. He then walks to the lounge area at the front of the house and dials Paisley.

Within one ring, she responds. "Tommy, are you okay? Is Lancy okay? What happened? Oh, I've been so worried."

"I'm fine, Paise. Listen, I need to stay here for a few more hours, until her mum comes home. It was really frightening—I pretty much broke into the house, found a suicide letter she left for her mum, and then found her in the bath, already drowned. She killed herself. I don't how I was lucky enough to revive her."

"Oh, my God, Tom! That is so frightening. I'm so glad you revived her. Yes, it's best that you stay with her, and don't tell her mum. What is she doing now?"

"She is fast asleep at the moment. Her mother gets home at 6:00 a.m., so I'll leave around 5:30. I'll see how she is in a couple of hours. Who knows, I may leave earlier. I'm sorry, Paisley."

"No; Tom, it's perfectly fine. I totally understand that you need to be there for her, especially right now. I remember how tough it can get."

"Okay, I'd better go. I'll go keep my eye on her. I'll see you in the morning, Paise."

"Okay. I love ya, Tommy. Keep safe."

Back in Laney's room, he sets his alarm to go off at 5:00 a.m., and he then places the phone on the dressing table at the foot of the bed. He sits on the chair that is part of the décor of the dressing table, borrows Laney's pen and scrap paper, and writes a note.

> *Dearest Janey,*
>
> *When you awaken from your slumber, you will find that I have already left. I'm sure you understand why I left: the confrontation with your mother and me wouldn't be viable. I want you to know that I slept beside you and held you until five in the morning. You can call me or text me whenever you feel you need to. I'll be sure this time that I will answer it. You are such a beautiful girl, Janey. The world, and*

> *even life itself, wouldn't be worth existing without*
> *you here. I just want to let you know that I know*
> *you love me like* Romeo and Juliet, *and I love—*

A loud scream emanating from Laney startles him, disrupting his note.

"No, Tom, don't leave. Please don't leave me." He drops the pen to the floor and he leaps towards the bed, once again caressing her. From the nightmare, Laney has now turned over to face him.'

"Tom-Tom, I love you so much. You wanna marry me? I want you to be mine forever." Upon hearing her mumbles, his eyebrows rise in surprise, even though he knows she is sleep talking.

With her brittle, naked body pressed against his, he feels the perkiness of her breasts brush his chest. Her leg suddenly crosses over his waist. Upon straightening out his body, he turns on his back so her leg isn't raised as high. In search of a more comfortable zone, she rests her bent leg just above his lower stomach. His hand now rests against her lower regions, brushing her vagina with each waggle she makes.

Laying stagnant and gazing at the off-white paint applied to the ceiling isn't presenting him any sort of direction whatsoever. The idea of knowing there is a naked girl sleeping over him will not fade any time soon. His erection is robust, and it aches from the pressure of being confined in the stiffness of his underwear. He's incapable of moving his hand away from her genitalia, and the urge worsens by the minute. Any slight movement he makes can cause a sense of elation towards her.

In an attempt to clear his mind, he scopes the room to notice a lamp that was switched on earlier. To the right of the room, two large doors hide the wardrobe. Shifting his attention, he spots a clock with a dark orange butterfly that looks to be flying sideways at a hasty rate. At first glance, this picture resembles the artwork cover from the Prince album *For You*.

The time on this unique clock displays 11:11 p.m. In surprise, his eyes widen from the suspicious beliefs of the mystical powers those numbers carry. Suddenly he recalls Paisley demanding that when those numbers appear visible to the naked eye, it means the angels are watching over them.

Laney begins moving about in her sleep. He tries remaining as still as he possibly can. Searching for the warmth of his skin, she moves her face in to his, resting her lips on his cheek. Her delicious aroma resembles a scent of vanilla. He inhales a deepened breath, and then in angst, he turns the other way, displaying his back to her.

In his attempt to turn over, Laney manages to wrap her leg around him, to force him flat on his back again. Resting on his back won't allow him to sleep, so he tries turning on his side to face her.

Finally reaching his comfort zone, he can't help but marvel at her beautiful face. With sincerity, he smiles whilst gazing at her closed eyes. Unexpectedly, he too feels his own eyes beginning to slowly close. Each blink becomes heavier, and the vanilla scent is no longer tasty; it's more a soothing scent now. The feeling of nirvana is rapidly approaching him. Holding his hand out to the reverie, he finally grasps it to enter into his slumber.

CHAPTER 36

It's That Time

The annoying sounds of his alarm rudely awaken him in a fright. In a bewildered state, he desperately sits up and taps the screen to stop the alarm. As he does, his mind adjusts to where he was, and he looks to the opposite side of him to find an empty spot in the bed. Feeling the cold draft in the room, he looks down to his bare chest to realise his top is missing. Upon raising the sheet, he unexpectedly perceives that his underwear is the only means of protection of his private property.

"What the hell happened?" he asks himself. "Where's Lancy?" In a distant part of the home, he hears the flushing of a toilet.

"Shit!" He searches the room for his clothing. Finally, he spots the dressing table displaying his pants and his top, which have been folded and placed neatly over the chair. He rapidly throws on his pants, and before he is able to place his arm into his top, Lancy enters the room wearing a tight pink singlet accompanied with a cute pair of red skimpy underwear. It's enticing to the eyes, and he can't help but stand marvelling at her.

"Hey, my Tom-Tom is finally awake!" she says, hopping onto him and wrapping her legs around his waist. After kissing him vigorously over his cheeks, and forehead, she senses anger within him as he lowers her to the ground, aggressively pulling away from her.

"Janey, why were my clothes off?" he asks in distress.

"What? You don't remember?" she says with a flirtatious smile.

"Remember what, Janey? What did we do?"

She giggles and says, "*We* do? No, Tom, just I did!"

He shakes his head, trying to remain as calm as he can. "Janey, please tell me what happened."

"You seriously don't recall anything at all?"

"No, and you can see I don't! Now, please tell me what happened."

"Well, we had sex, Tom."

"What?" he screams loudly, almost piercing her ear drums.

"What's the matter? You didn't like it?"

With pure adrenaline, he crashes his hand over the dressing table to respond, "I didn't want it to happen, Janey! That's what the matter is! Fuck!"

"Calm down, will you? Jesus! You made me do everything anyway; you just laid there and waited to cum inside me."

"What the fuck?" he screams even louder. "How could you let that happen, Janey?"

"You're the one who did it Tom. You started touching me, putting your fingers inside me. And I've been wanting it badly, so I accepted and let you continue. I can't believe you're getting so angry over this! I knew you fucking hated me, Tom."

He swings his arm with all his might, slapping Janey across the face and instantly knocking her to the floor. As he bends to tend to her, the sound of an alarm awakens him.

In fright and in a pool of sweat, he shakes his head in disbelief. He finds that he has just woken from sleep, which leads him to forget the time he set his alarm for. As he grasps his phone, he notes the time reads 5:01 a.m. He then looks to the opposite side of him to find Lancy, lying on her side and facing the other way. Thankfully, he is still covered in his clothing. Knowing he needs to leave soon, he slowly creeps out of the bed, trying his best not to wake her. Then he covers her exposed body with the blanket.

After relieving his filled bladder, he quickly washes up and then heads back into the bedroom to check on Lancy. She's fast asleep in dream land, so he kisses her on the cheek. Then he hears a beeping sound from in the kitchen. With haste, he heads there to find Lancy's phone lit up. He notices a message from 0468952367. Realising that the time is only 5:13 a.m., his curiosity gets the better of him, so he swipes the message to read it.

> Hey, Lancy. I am fully aware that you will be sleeping right now! I actually can't believe I'm messaging you so early in the morning, but I haven't been able to sleep. The reason is I can't stop thinking about you. I know this may sound so abrupt and rushed.

Tom stops reading because his thoughts overpower the message. He mutters to himself, "It's probably Jacob." Then he continues reading.

"I really want to see you again. I've only seen you this once today, and Lancy, it's as though I got a taste of something so sweet, so delicious, and then had it taken away from me.

"This can't be Jacob," he mutters to himself.

I need to take you out! If I don't write this message to you now, I won't sleep a wink. So please call me or message me back, because I saw something in you, I saw me being with you.

Josh

"Josh! Who is this Josh? Is she lying to me? Is she seeing someone?" He thinks the worst. "How am I to leave here, knowing this message has unexpectedly appeared? Do I wake her up? This is not going to let me concentrate on anything today. Why did she not tell me about this Josh? I cannot fathom it. I am so disappointed … I've gotta wake her up."

He marches to her bedroom in a heated manner. Upon walking into the room, he finds that she has turned to face the other way. Snuggled up in her bed, she looks so peaceful. Interrupting her now will ruin the beauty she exhibits.

As he heads towards her, he freezes suddenly, hearing the front door open. Afraid to confront her mother, he remains oblivious on what his escape plan will be. The first noticeable escape route is the window in her bedroom, but it's far too small to climb out of it. Recalling the two large doors hiding the wardrobe, he hastily opens them up to find that he may actually fit inside it. After forcing himself in, he ducks behind her clothes and then closes the doors the best he can behind him.

Footsteps soon appear inside the bedroom, and then a soft voice says, "Oh, my Jane! My poor baby, I haven't seen you at all lately!" He peeks through the crack of the doors and spots a woman who he thinks is Lancy's mother. She kneels in prayer beside the bed, caressing Lancy's head, and says, "I promise I will try my hardest to take some time off to spend with you, my girl. I'm going to be here for you the best I can." Upon hearing no response from Lancy, he gathers she is fast asleep and hasn't heard a single word.

As soon as the mother exits the bedroom, he presses his ear to the door, heeding any movements she can make. Suddenly, a glass door slams loudly enough to attract his ear. Then soon after, there's the sound of flowing water. Sensing an opportunity, he hurriedly storms out, closing the doors behind him. Then he stands vertically in guard of Lancy.

In her ear, he whispers delicately, "I love you. I love you in the tree-engraving way, Jancy Lane." He then leans in and presses his lips over hers. Whilst admiring her scent, he holds the kiss momentarily, resting his cheek against hers.

CHAPTER 37

Some More Time to Think

At 6:03 a.m., the apartment is in lockdown mode. The ambience is completely inaudible. The darkness throughout the room gives Tom no option of any visibility, until after a minute or so, where his eyes finally adjust to the surroundings.

He heads toward Paisley's room to find it vacant. Somewhat startled, his next option is his bedroom. Upon entering through a half-closed door, he finds her on his bed fast asleep, caressing his pillow. After shutting the door behind him, he makes his way to the lounge area.

While seated on the sofa in the same spot where he made love to Paisley, images of the sexual encounter circulate throughout his mind. He tries to ignore it and presses the standby button, switching on the television. Without bothering to surf the stations, he leaves on the channel broadcasting a familiar film to him.

I can't believe I gave into Paisley the way I did. I should not have let that happen. She was aware of the agreement we made together, and she was aware that my temptation will get the better of me. I'm so bloody weak … Thankfully, she is unable to fall pregnant. That could've been a complete disaster. How the hell am I to tell Janey?

Do I even need to tell Janey? What am I saying? Janey is far too young for me, and it's completely wrong. Who is this Josh? I really need to ask her about that ... *I'm so tired, yet I know I won't be able to sleep. What is this film? Jim Carrey and Kate Winslet* ... *Yes, I know this film:* Eternal Sunshine of the Spotless Mind. *What a coincidence!* He quietly chuckles and then looks to the clock over by the wall: 6:37 a.m. *I think I'll just keep watching this film, and see if it helps me fall asleep* ...Moments later he finally caves into a deep sleep.

CHAPTER 38

Waking to an Empty Bed

After waking in a semi fright, the ceiling is Laney's first view. Next is the empty spot beside her. She bangs her hand over the bed, noticing the time on the butterfly clock. Remaining unclothed, she stampedes through the house to find her phone resting on the kitchen table. Upon grasping it, she recalls the suicide note and sighs loudly.

"Shit! I hope Mum hasn't got it. Is Mum even home? I can't believe he just left me here. He bloody left me again!"

She heads towards her mother's bedroom and finds that its vacant. With her phone resting in her palm, she swipes the screen to send a text message. Upon swiping, she notices a message that was left on the screen.

"What the hell?" she mutters loudly, remaining oblivious to the message itself. "Did Mum read this? Why would she have read it? She never goes through my phone … I can't believe Tom fucking left me again." Abruptly her anger turned to tears, watching several drops land over the screen of her phone as she searches for her mother through the contacts.

"I gotta text them both." Undecided on whom she should text first, Tom appears before her mother on her list. "I can't be upset at Tom. I don't want to push him away! So, Lancy, be nice …"

She writes, "Hi, Tom-Tom. I was desperately looking for you when I woke up, but you weren't there. That made me really sad. Can you please call me ASAP? I love you …" Upon pressing send, she types the next message to her mother.

"Hey, Mum, how are you? Is everything okay? I missed you again. I want to see you. Can we please try to make a time to see each other? And did you look at my phone, by any chance?"

She heads to the toilet and keeps refreshing her phone, hoping Tom will respond. After she relieves her bladder, she recalls the message from the undisclosed number to realise it was Josh. "Oh, shit! Who looked at my phone?"

A text notification from her mother appears on the screen. "Hey, honey. I had to go back into work—they really needed me. I feel so bad. I miss you so much. I'm going to try to make some time that we can spend together. No, I didn't touch your phone; you know I don't touch your phone. I've gotta go. Call me if you need anything. Love you."

So it wasn't Mum. At what time was this message sent? She scrolls through the messages. "At 5:13 a.m. What the hell? Maybe Tom was still here … Why isn't he responding? Fuck! Why is Josh texting me so early, anyway?" She continues with the remainder of the message. "Oh, okay, well, get in line, Josh, because I can't stop thinking about your dad. He is going to be the death of me."

Seated lazily and unclothed over the sofa with her legs crossed, she strangles the phone in her sweaty palm, awaiting a response from Tom. Her eyes finally drift away from the screen to the television. Unexpectedly, the phone beeps. Her fingers go on a frenzy, swiping as fast as she can.

Tom's message reads, "Hi, Laney. How are you feeling?"

Disconcertedly, she says to herself, *That's it? That's all he writes? He never calls me Laney!* Hurriedly she replies, "Not so good, Tom. Can we meet today—actually as soon as you can?"

"I can't sweetie!"

What the fuck? "Sweetie?" She is in anguish.

He continues. "I have so much to do today. I'll try to speak to you at a later date."

Is he going crazy? Why is he doing this to me? Why? She howls as she tosses the phone to the floor. After bawling her eyes out, she suddenly collapses to the floor of the kitchen. "I wish he didn't save me. I'm so sorry, Adam. I should've just come to you when you gave me the chance. You were right all along …"

CHAPTER 39

The Narrator

Hi. I must leave this scene for a brief moment. Tom has a much more significant scene. It's fine, because Lancy will keep sobbing for a while longer …

CHAPTER 40

Tom

From the toilet, Tom walks into the lounge area undetected and spots Paisley in her underwear and sports bra. She's bent over the bench and hovering over an object. While admiring her skimpy underwear creeping up the cheeks of her buttocks, he sneakily creeps up to her to perceive her snooping at his phone.

In a startling manner, she drops the phone against the bench and then says, "Hey, baby. You're awake?"

He defensively responds, "Is that my phone, Paise?"

With a look of innocence, she brushes her hand across his face, adjusting his hair. Then she responds, "Yeah, I was just looking at it."

With a sense of petulance, he grabs the phone and then heads to his room. The home screen is notification free, so he checks his messages to observe the last message that was sent to Lancy.

From the kitchen area, he hears Paisley yell out, "Hey, I'm making breakfast. What would you like to eat, baby?"

He scrolls through the messages, perceiving what Paisley had written on his behalf. "What the hell?" he mutters to himself. "I've gotta call her now." He makes several attempts to call her, but there is no response from her end.

CHAPTER 41

Back to Laney

Laney lies stark naked over the cold floor, tears oozing from her eyes, endlessly dripping to the floor and creating a puddle deep enough to dip the full of her fingernail into it.

Her body feels heavy, as though there is this king-size mattress placed over the top of her. With all her strength, she tries raising herself off the cold floor and make her way into the bathroom in an attempt to fill up the bathtub. This unforeseen hefty weight over her body is making it impossible for her to raise herself up. She determinedly begins to creep in, dragging her naked body over the cold tiles. It feels as though a powerful force is holding her back. Anxious to fight off this force, she continues dragging her flaccid body till she finally reaches the bathroom. Upon hearing a vibrating sound from in the lounge area, she halts momentarily but then apathetically chooses to ignore it.

Having reached her destination, her body feels heavier than it did minutes ago. With great strength, she raises her body just enough to turn the faucet so as to fill up the bath. The length of her stretch only allows for her to reach the cold faucet; at this time, hot water is of no concern to her.

Her next mission is lifting her weight high enough to enter the bathtub. Through what she thought may be an absolute impossibility, she manages to slide into the bath but bangs her head against the faucet in the process. The knock was very painful but doesn't concuss her.

Upon finally resting her head against the back of the bath, in a sudden sense of shock, she notices the water slowly turning red. With her right hand, she scoops the water up to see the pool of blood fall from her palm.

In this lifeless state, she can't help but shiver as she lies helpless in a pool of cold blood. The room suddenly becomes a little hazy. *Could be the running water,* she admits to herself, but the haze is blackening to a point where darkness is quickly replacing her sight. Through the darkness, she hears a banging sound resonating from the other side of the home. The sound is heard but is of no concern to her, due to her eyes being far too heavy for her to remain in control of them. Quickly, her consciousness is fading …

CHAPTER 42

Hope I'm Not Too Late

$\mathcal{M}$iraculously, Tom feels fortunate to find the door left open, and he walks straight into the home. In distress, he slams the door shut behind him, and then he spots Lancy's phone resting on the floor in the lounge. He scopes the entire house before he finally hears the sound of water running from in the bathroom. Upon entering the bathroom, his eyes perceive Lancy floating in a bath filled with blood, with her head resting by the side while the water still runs.

He quickly turns off the water, grasping her body to raise her out of the bath. With his ear pressed to her mouth, he perceives her slow breaths. After laying her over an unmade bed, he notices her pale skin before and so throws several blankets over her body. Lancy shivers vigorously from the coldness she has just endured. He places his ear over her mouth, hoping that she is still breathing.

Her breaths are at the right pace, but the colour of her skin isn't changing. Unsure about what he needs to do, he decides to pick her up and hold her in his arms. As he does, he observes the blood on the blanket and then searches her body to see where it is coming from. After a thorough search, he finally spots the open gash on her head. He places the blanket over the gash, applying as much pressure as he can to stop the flow of blood.

After two long minutes of holding her in his arms, he stares at her unconscious state and then places his lips gently against hers. They are as cold as they look. He applies pressure against her lips to offer the warmth of his. He feels her eyelashes flicker against his cheek. Then she finally opens her eyes and says, "Ouch!" He smiles in gratitude and watches her expression hurriedly change. "Tom, what happened? Did I upset you again?"

He shakes his head at her in distress. "Jancy, no. It wasn't me who was responding to the messages. I told you I wouldn't do that to you again."

"What do you mean?" she asks in a shivering state. Her words are undistinguishable from the severity of her quiver.

He removes his top to expose his chest against her naked torso, offering the heat she yearns for. Instantly, she embraces the warmth. After several minutes of offering his body heat, he asks, "What did you do, Jancy? How did you hurt your head?"

She pulls her head back to gaze at him and then responds, "It was weird. My body felt really heavy. I could barely crawl, which is what I did to get into the bathroom. And because I was so weak, as I got into the bath, I banged my head. It was accidental … Why did you leave me, Tom? You knew the state I was in. Why would you leave me?"

"Did you not see the note on your dressing table?" he says, pointing in that direction.

"No, I didn't. I woke up in a panic when I didn't see you or my mum. And I didn't know how to react. I got confused and overwhelmed, and then I tried contacting you. I got these ridiculous responses …"

He hushes to silence her. "I'm so, so sorry, Janey! I never meant for this to happen to you. I needed to get out of the house before your mum got home, and that is what I wrote in the note."

Suddenly she recalls the note she left on the table and asks, "Oh, Tom, did you take the note I left for Mum?"

"Yes, I did."

"Oh, good!" With her index finger to her lip, she asks, "Hey, did you by any chance look at my phone?"

CHAPTER 43

The Narrator

This one scene, right here, becomes very awkward for the both of them. Obviously, Tom refrains from responding immediately due to the fact that he doesn't want her thinking he is a snooper—you know, the type who needs to check a partner's phone. On the other hand, Lancy desperately needs questions answered. But in saying this, she doesn't want him to know that it was his son Josh. Now, back to the scene …

CHAPTER 44

Continued . . .

I mustn't lie to her. It's not right. I cannot possibly start this friendship that way.

He responds. "I did. I heard it vibrate as I was about to leave your home. Of course, I was curious as to why it vibrated. Then I noticed a random number on their stating you had a message. I swiped it to see who it was, out of curiosity because it was so early in the morning. I read the message and asked myself who this Josh person was. Then your mum startled me by coming home. I left the phone with the message open and hid in the wardrobe.

"Now, one important thing that has got me speculating is who this Josh could be. And why is he messaging you at five in the morning?"

After laughing loudly at him, she tries hiding the deceitfulness that her emotions are displaying.

"Why are you laughing?" he asks.

Continuing to chuckle, she responds, "I pictured you trying to escape from my mum and hiding in my wardrobe. It's very funny, Tom."

"I didn't find it funny. Can you please tell me who this Josh is?"

Gazing at his smile, she brushes her thumb over the full of his lips. He smiles at her and then gazes at her hair and her weary eyes. Despite having almost died for the second time, she still manages to look as beautiful as ever. He's totally aware she is avoiding responding to his infamous question, and he chooses to momentarily leave it be while he admires the beauty standing in front of him. Once her thumb flicks off his lips, he watches her as she gazes deeply into his eyes—a gaze that calls upon him with an expression of desire.

Shaking his head vigorously, he demands, "Janey, I really need to know who this josh is."

She responds, "I'll tell you after this …" She moves forward and into him with pouted lips.

He watches as she edges closer towards him, gazing immensely at the voluptuousness of her lips. He then shifts back and forth from her closed eyes to her lips.

Upon contact, her mouth opens slightly, smearing the dampness of her inner lips against his. Her taste is delightful. He licks her lips with his tongue, yearning for more of her taste. With the strength of her lips, she persists in trying to open his mouth to greet his tongue. When he's unresponsive to her persistence, she bites on his lips. Desiring the taste of the interior of her mouth, he finally gives in, offering his tongue to her. She accepts the intrusion with open arms, allowing it to enter into her mouth.

Having found a new home, both tongues admire the surroundings and the taste that comes with it. Fortunately, he finds that she still possesses the vanilla scent that he craved earlier on. Their mouths work to a point where Laney desires something greater.

She pushes him over onto the bed and then sits comfortably on top of him. Unprotected, the dampness from her lower regions marks his jeans where she sits. She impassively rubs her already wet crotch against his sheltered erection, staining the jeans in the process. Sensing the erection protruding from the protection of his jeans, she presses her body weight harder against it.

Leaning down to his chest, she kisses his nipples and then slowly makes her way down to his pants, skilfully unzipping his jeans. With hurried reflexes, he places his hands over his jeans in an attempt to disrupt her. She leaves the pants momentarily, making her way up to his mouth again and frolicking with his tongue. Within this deed, she slides his jeans down in a proficient manner, somehow without disrupting his chain of thought. Back to his chest, she licks around his nipples whilst peeking up at him with a smile, hoping she is performing the way he imagined. Finally, she grasps his limp hands that rest by his waist, placing them over her breasts. His touch instantly sends a shiver down her spine, forcing her to shake her body in the process. The sense of his touch and his skin against hers—she has been yearning for this moment since he rescued her from her first suicide attempt.

With his jeans resting below his thighs, all she needs to do now is to remove his underwear. She peeks at his underwear, admiring the force his penis is presenting as it battles to escape the confinement.

Without making any eye contact with him, she grabs the shaft of his penis through his underwear, squeezing it and then tickling the head. Quivering with desire, his eyes roll back to into his skull.

After noticing the desire he is enduring, she removes his underwear. Upon the initial exposing, she gives a giggle whilst admiring the erectness of the penis and how it is able to point to the heavens in such a miraculous way. The erection he endures is explosive; he could almost ejaculate from the erection itself.

She glances at it before she decides on placing her hand around the shaft, somewhat teasing it with a couple of slow strokes. Incapable of removing her eyes from it, she finally finds the strength and then looks deeply into his eyes. They gaze upon each other passionately, in a way where together, they understand the love they feel for each other. She smiles an innocent grin and then quickly refocuses on the hard penis that packs the whole of her hand.

Unaware of what to do, she continues stroking delicately. Then she leans down toward his penis. Only inches away from her face, she giggles at the size and then relishes at the thought of what it will taste like. She leisurely continues stroking it, almost in a teasing fashion. Finally, she opens her mouth and then licks his genitals as a cat will do from a milk bowl. From there, she begins tickling the exposed meatus with her thumb, wondering what is under the foreskin.

After she has one last gaze at his droopy eyes, she remains curious as to what his penis tastes like, so she licks at the exposed tip of the meatus, instantly causing quivers down his spine. Admiring the taste, she licks again, wanting to place her lips around it.

Tom unexpectedly gathers her up, wanting to taste her

mouth again. They passionately re-embark on another journey of this freshly discovered taste they both relish so desperately. With a hint of aggression, he places his fingers at her crotch, noticing the dampness of her lower regions. He then carries her over him, hovering her vagina over the stiffness of his penis. He raises his pelvis gently, rubbing his throbbing penis against the opening of her vagina. He watches as she quivers in ecstasy, and she raises her waist, leaving the penis homeless. In a sudden sense of shock, she questions the hurt she may feel when the full length of penis enters inside her. But at the same time, she yearns desperately for it.

With their hands caressing one another's faces, they passionately continue smooching till finally he raises his pelvis in search of the insertion point. Her body tingles as it rubs against her vagina. Slowly and precisely, he lowers her body onto his penis. The guidance is the cleanest and smoothest he has ever felt.

As it inserts inside her, she halts hastily as she felt the pain of his enormous penis breaking through her vaginal opening. Together they moan in ecstasy as the full length is fully inserted. With a sense of frenzy, she drops her head back, relishing the euphoria. Within the first motion she applies, the pain quickly eases and rapidly turns into pleasure.

Having formed a rhythm, she continues motioning back and forth, pushing the penis deeply inside her. Her moans are almost ear piercing, and the tightness within her vagina is proof enough that she was indeed a virgin. He watched the deepness within her and the sight of her elation, his ejaculation is approaching steadily. He rests the weight of his hands upon her waist to somewhat slow her down. She shrugs his hands away, motioning in every direction possible. She then squeezes her legs hard against his waist, screaming, "Tom? I think I'm cumming!"

Suddenly she starts moving harder and faster, taking full control of his hands and demanding they squeeze her breasts. She screams from the top of her lungs, and he watches her move back and forth, resting her hand over his chest and admiring the sheer darkness she perceives whilst relishing the orgasm she is experiencing in a shivering sweat.

As she undergoes this experience of reaching a full climax, he sits admiring her beauty as he gazes at her eyes, watching a tear drop to his chest. He smiles in gratification whilst slowly thrusting. Once her eyes finally open, her body shivers from ecstasy as his thrusts jolt her wilted body back and forth.

Content that she was able to experience her first orgasm, he decides on applying his own brand by flipping her over and laying her on her back. His penis withdraws as the turn occurs, so he guides it back in with the use of his pelvis. She moans loudly upon insertion and then rests her hands over his buttocks, squeezing them to push him deeper inside her.

With every thrust applied, her moans appear louder and louder. She senses another climax approaching rapidly as he thrusts deeper and deeper. Undoubtedly, he feels his orgasm swiftly approaching, and so he says to Lancy, "Jancy, I am at the point of ejaculating."

Ignoring his request, she keeps moaning with every thrust and holds him into her. "No! It feels so good. Please don't stop …"

The temptation is far too overpowering. He tries applying

pressure to pull himself out, but with remarkable strength she manages to hold him into her, forcing him to ejaculate deep inside her.

Upon doing so, she screams louder than she did earlier, climaxing for the second time. He shivers as she keeps moving her pelvis up and down over his worn-out penis. After resting his face against her, he whispers into her ear, "I love you, Jancy!"

In that instance, when Lancy hears Tom speak from his heart, she sheds a tear. "I love you so much more …"

CHAPTER 45

Just a Few Questions

Feebly resting naked in the bed after a long, lasting sexual encounter, Tom turns away from the ceiling to face Laney. He says, "Janey,; I need a few questions answered."

With a look of confusion, she responds, "Okay."

He already has a sense of the answer, but he asks, "Am I your first?"

Blushing, she responds, "Of course, Tommy. Didn't you notice I didn't know what I was doing? But I'm so happy that my first time was with you, with the person I love. I know a lot of girls who have done it with random people, and they regretted it. Boy, am I glad I wasn't one of them."

While combing her hair with his fingers, he smiles and then uncivilly asks, "Are you on any kind of contraception?"

She smirks and then responds, "No! I never thought that I'd ever need them, because no one ever loved me … Do I need it now?"

"Yes, of course you do, Janey. I just ejaculated inside of you."

"Yes, I know—and I loved it."

He shakes his head and furiously continues. "Janey, you

must go and get the morning-after pill, because you may fall pregnant from this."

Still giggling, she adds, "It's okay, Tom-Tom. I think I'm getting my period in a week or so. Leave it with me, and I'll sort it all out."

"This is serious, Jancy! You cannot fall pregnant."

"Shh ..." She hushes him with his finger over his lips. "I said I'll sort all of this out. I won't fall pregnant."

Having accepted her word, he says, "Okay. My final question is, who is this Jo ...?"

His phone unexpectedly rings to interrupt him. He abruptly turns to face the bedside table, only to realise it is Paisley calling him. He looks to Lancy and says, "I need to take this!" He then hops out of the bed, walking to the entrance of the bedroom. After having exited the room, he says, "Paise!"

"Hey, baby! How is it going? How is Lancy? Is she okay?"

"She is fine! I can't really speak at the moment, because I'm still with her."

"Well, I want you to come home."

"Okay, I will soon. Just let me finish up with Janey." With his back facing the bedroom, he doesn't notice Lancy until she brushes him as she storms past him. "Paise, I gotta go." He hangs up the phone to chase Lancy, managing to grasp her forearm before she can enter the toilet. "Jancy, stop!"

"No, Tom! I have a bad feeling about this Paisley relationship ..."

"Jancy, I don't want you to get worked up over this. It's nothing."

"What's nothing to you, Tom, means everything to me.

I feel it in my stomach that the story with Paisley is not as simple as it seems."

"I will not discuss this right now with you!"

"Why not? Are you hiding something from me, Tom?"

He slaps the wall and says, "Janey, please. I don't want to do this now. Don't make me tell you again."

"Fine! Go to your Paisley. Don't keep her waiting," she says, shrugging off the grip he has on her forearm. She storms back into her bedroom.

Following her lead, he says, "Janey, I need to go. Are you going to be okay?"

She gathers the appropriate clothing to carry with her in the bathroom. Before she exits the bedroom, she says, "Yes, Tom. Can you at least meet me later on? Maybe after you do Paisley?"

"Janey, enough! I am not leaving for Paisley. Just … I'll call you later."

Without watching him leave, she hears the thud of the door shutting as he exits the house. Then she bangs her hand on the bathroom door, screaming, "Fuck!"

CHAPTER 46

Josh

$\mathcal{F}$ifteen minutes after Tom left her home, she finds her phone to bring up Josh's message and read it again. Then she replies, "Hi, Josh. Wow! You really couldn't sleep? I guess I slept well because I failed to hear the message you sent me at 5:00 a.m. What the hell were you thinking? I mean, are you crazy texting me at that time?" After pressing send, she places her phone over the kitchen table and then heads back to her bedroom to sit on the chair at her dressing table. She finally notices the note Tom left for her. Through the course of reading over the note, she can't help but think about Paisley.

I'm sure he is hiding something from me with that Paisley. I mean, why is he so protective of her?

Her phone unexpectedly beeps, interrupting her chain of thought. The message is from Josh. "Hey, Lancy. I'm so sorry I texted you so early, but I needed to tell you how I truly felt. I need to see you. Can I see you?"

She looks to the clock on the wall and notes that she has time on her hands. She responds, "That's all good. Sure, I'll meet you. How about I come to your place, and we go from there?"

His reply is instant. "That's fantastic! My address is 46 Crescent Drive, Thornbury. When will you be here?"

"I'll leave now. I know exactly where that is, which isn't far. I'll see you soon."

CHAPTER 47

At Josh's House

$\mathcal{L}$ancy finds herself standing at the front door of Josh's home. She scopes the street, questioning herself whether this is the right thing she is doing. Disregarding the visions of Tom, she knocks on the door.

Under a minute later, a beautiful woman answers, leaving Lancy at awe with the beauty that stands before her.

"Hi, there. You must be Lancy. I'm Simone."

Offering her hand, Lancy humbly responds, "Yes, that's me. I'm, um, here to see …"

"Josh. Yes, I am aware of that. Come in, and I'll fetch him for you." As Lancy enters, Simone points to the sofa, requesting for her to take a seat. She does so welcomingly and hurriedly scopes the room, admiring the furniture.

Dressed in black Nike track pants and a label T-shirt of some sort, Josh says, "So where would you like to go, Lancy?"

She says, "Josh; your mother is beautiful …"

Peering into the kitchen, he responds, "Really? I don't really look at my mum that way. But I'm sure she would be delighted that you said that."

"I am not kidding. She needs to be told how beautiful she is."

Through her persistence, he begins laughing uncontrollably at her. "I'm sure she is, Lancy, but are you aware of how beautiful *you* are?"

Her serious grin turns to a blush. Somewhat uncomfortable, she responds, "Not as beautiful as your mother."

"I beg to differ, Lancy. You are exquisite."

Still blushing, she watches Simone enter into the room and say, "He is right, Lancy. You are a beautiful girl. And thank you for your kind words."

Lancy watches her exit the room, and she looks to Josh and asks, "Hey, and your dad—is he working?"

With angst, Josh shakes his head. "My dad works—"

Before he is able to speak anymore, Simone hurriedly re-enters the room and says, "His dad is probably working, yes. Josh, don't say anything you're going to regret, honey. Lancy, Tom and I separated a long time ago; he no longer lives here."

"Mum! Can you not do this in front of her, please?"

Lancy intervenes. "No, it's fine. I understand his anger. My father walked out on my mum and me a long time ago." With a diligent stare, she asks Simone, "Simone, may I be blunt?"

"Sure, Lancy. Speak your mind."

"Are you still in love with your ex-husband?"

Josh bangs his hand over the sofa. "I cannot believe we are talking about this shit!"

Simone says, "Hush, Josh! Lancy, I never fell out of love with Tom. He fell out of love with me. I still long for the day he returns to this family."

Instantly Lancy's heart sinks. She is lost for words till Josh steps in and says, "Are we doing this, Lancy, or what?"

Sensing Josh's frustration, Simone says, "I think Josh is getting a little anxious. Go have a nice day, you two."

Lancy stands and offers her hand to Simone. "Simone, it was a pleasure to have met you … I hope we can see each other again soon."

Josh grabs Lancy's arm to drag her out of the house.

CHAPTER 48

Brandon on the Line

"So, who is this next client, my friend?"

"Unfortunately, another teenager. We have been flooded with calls from so many teenagers lately. It's frightening."

"I agree. I actually feel sick in the stomach to realise that there are so many teenagers feeling that they have nothing left, and so they resort to this."

"Yes, it is sickening, I'm afraid! Paisley tells me that you and Lancy are progressing well?"

Tom hesitates and then says, "Yes. There has been the occasion where she has needed me, because she goes through these … well, I'm sure you are aware of what they go through."

"Yes—yes, I am. She too is concerned about you, Paisley. That is …"

"Paisley's involvement sometimes isn't required as much as she claims she needs it to be."

"Well, you are aware of her feelings, I'm sure."

"Indeed I am … I'm just going through a lot at the moment, especially with my son becoming one of my clients."

"I'm so sorry, Tom. I didn't know what else to do with Josh."

"No, I'm not having a go at you, my friend. I'm simply stating the obvious."

"Okay, well, I'm pleased to hear it was resolved with him."

"Yes, me too."

"It's been a pleasure conversing with you. I have the client's details in my drop box. Have a nice day, my friend."

"You too."

CHAPTER 49

What Is the Story with Your Dad?

Josh rests his hand over the counter, waiting to pay for the two lattes he ordered for the two of them. Seated at the table by the window, Laney can't help but gaze at society around her. Interrupting her gaze, Josh finally seats himself down in front of her, handing her a Mars bar–flavoured macaroon to indulge in. She spins the plate, circling the radius of the macaroon whilst admiring his kind gesture.

"What a gentleman!" she says with a smile.

"Have you tasted these, Laney? It's my favourite."

"No, I can't say that I have." Offering assistance, he gathers the fork that rests beside the macaroon to cut a piece for her. With a saddened expression, she says, "Josh, I am so sorry! I can't eat that macaroon"

"Why is that? I mean, you haven't even tried it."

"I'm actually gluten intolerant."

"Oh, you're kidding me! I'm so sorry, I wasn't aware of that. I'll go ask if they have anything else."

Before he is able to get up off his chair, she says, "No, Josh!

— 161 —

It's fine. I've been here many times, and they have nothing for me. And just so you are aware, I'm a real coeliac—not those fake types where they claim they are intolerant and then go snack on bread and donuts. I will get sick if I have anything containing gluten, and that's that. I'm actually used to it. Trust me, it's okay. You eat it, and I'll watch you indulge in it." She laughs.

Moments later, the coffees finally arrive. She perceives a heart created within the froth. Smiling at it, she looks in the direction of the barista, who is a young female who hasn't even noticed Laney looking her way. She asks, "Josh, can I ask you a personal question? Feel free to tell me to get lost, if you choose not to respond."

"Sure, what is it?"

She sips the coffee and admires the creamy taste. Then she asks, "What is the story with your dad? Like, why did he leave at such a young age?"

He shrugs his shoulders whilst glancing down at his coffee. Then finally he says, "To tell you the truth, I'm still not 100 per cent sure on what actually happened. I hold a lot of hatred towards my father, and I just don't want to know."

"Okay, that's fine. I guess I understand."

With an immense stare, he circles the rim of the cup and then adds, "He was always too busy, Mum said. He quit his job and got this new one that was so secretive, where Mum only knew minor details. It was supposed to free him up a little more, but it didn't—it just got worse. The job my dad had previous to this one made him depressed, I think. He was doing it for a very long time, and it must've got the better of him. Be aware that I'm only going by what mum told me."

She nods in acknowledgement, prompting him to continue.

"Anyway, I'm not 100 per cent on this, but I think Dad may have cheated on Mum with a work colleague. Well, she sort of hinted that he did, but she never actually said it to my face."

"Oh, okay. Well, that explains a fair bit, actually!" she says, realising it may well be Paisley.

"Really?" he asks.

"Oh! Um, well, yeah." She realises she has said too much.

"How so?" he asks as he watches her fidgeting with her cup of coffee.

"Oh, well, I could tell by your mum's reactions when she spoke of your dad. I have that gift, I guess … So you don't know who the girl was, if there even was one?"

"No, I don't. Oh, actually, hold on. I think I may have overheard her mention a girl named Pai … something. I can't remember the name; it was a unique name."

"Right! Okay," she says in anguish.

CHAPTER 50

The Drop Box

Seated in his vehicle, Tom gazes at the envelope resting on the passenger seat. His usual gaze includes thoughts of a different nature. The cluster of thoughts is usually based upon the introduction of a new client. But this time, his mind is focused on one thing, one person, one love. This new envelope is invisible to him; he is unaware of how he even made it to the drop box to acquire it. That sex scene with Laney is far too memorable for him to focus on anything other than her. It repeats over and over, feeding him fuel to want it all over again. With his mind playing callous tricks on him, it's a constant battle with whether the sex with Laney was the right or wrong thing to do. The two parts of his mind separate from each other, purely for Tom to distinguish the positives and negatives of this new love for the sixteen-year-old.

His eyes suddenly perceive a holographic image of two columns, one titled positive and the other titled negative. He sees only the one negative in the column, and that is her age. The positives he views in this image are all in favour for him to make that one decision.

Once the image vanishes off the windscreen, he knows

his mind is set, and he is able to refocus on the envelope containing his next client. Using the same procedure, he opens the envelope, removing the folded paper that is perfectly placed inside it. As he flips over the paper, his phone beeps, forcing him to clumsily drop the paper to fall over the centre console. Upon tending to his phone, he notices it is from Paisley.

"Hey, baby. What are you up to? I haven't heard from you ... I really miss you, Are you okay?"

He inhales deeply whilst activating the keyboard. Mixed emotions clutter his mind, deeming him incapable of responding in the way he chooses to. In a disordered manner, he hovers his thumb over the screen in an attempt to respond. Then he types, "Hey, Paise. I miss y ..."

His phone beeps with a message from Lancy. Without hesitation, he swipes the message to read it. "Hey, Tom-Tom. I miss you, and I really need to see you and speak with you. I want to call you, but I'm not sure if you are with Paisley or not. I love you ..."

His initial thought is, *Why is she bringing up Paisley? She must know about us.* He accesses the keyboard to reply, "Hey, Jancy. I miss you too. I'm just tending to something at the moment. I'll call you as soon as I get the chance."

Upon clicking send, he switches back to Paisley's message, tweaking it. "Hey, Paise. I am busy at the moment. I'll call you when I get a chance."

Again his busy phone beeps—another message from Lancy. "What are you tending to, Tom? Are you with Paisley? Can I please call you?"

He anxiously dials her.

"Tom! Where are you? I need to see you now."

"I'm busy working, Janey."

"What are you doing that is so busy? You are always so discreet with me."

"Janey, I have a new client that I must tend to. Otherwise, I'll miss the meeting date."

"Who is the new client? Don't you think you should still be tending to me first?"

"It's not that simple, Janey! I have helped you to a point where I know you are safe."

"I understand, Tom … So you're not with Paisley?"

While feeling the vibration of another message coming through, he replies, "No, of course not! I'm in my car, trying to open up this next envelope."

"So you aren't in love with Paisley?"

"What? In love? What are you saying?"

Janey replies, "I don't even know what I'm saying. I'm going crazy, Tom. I need you to come see me so I can feel safe. Please come and see me. You can look at the envelope after you see me." He remains silent, deep in thought. "Tom? Are you there?"

"Yes. I'll be at your house in twenty minutes."

"Yes!" she says enthusiastically.

He chuckles at her enthusiasm and then says, "Did you fist-pump the air?"

"Hell yes, I did, Tom-Tom. I double fist-pumped. You should've seen them. I punched the air out of the air. You get it?"

He laughs and says, "Yes, I got it. I'll see you soon."

"Okay. I love you, Tom."

"I love you too."

Before he is able to disconnect the phone, he hears, "Tom, wait! Wait!"

"What's the matter, Jancy?" he asks.

"You said it back to me. You said you love me too. Did you hear yourself?"

He chuckles. "Yes, I heard myself. I'll see you in twenty minutes."

"Okay! Bye, my love."

CHAPTER 51

A Detour

While cruising at a comfortable speed, Tom's mind switches from despondency to a feeling of motivation as he relishes at the thought of arriving at a destination he so eagerly desires awaits. The phone disrupts his blissful thoughts, and he answers a call from Paisley.

"Paise, what's up?"

"Hi, baby. I was just sitting here, thinking about you and wondering why you haven't called me yet …"

"I just left the drop box."

"Oh, okay. You coming home now?"

"No. I'm actually on my way to Lancy's."

"Really? Didn't you just leave her an hour ago?"

"I did, but it was more than an hour."

She asks, "Why are you going back there again?"

Her question baffles him, leaving him sitting on the end of the line, desperate for a response. "This is what I do, Paise! If my clients require my services, I must be there for them. You should know this by now …"

"That's the problem, Tom. I *do* know. I know exactly what happened when I needed you."

"It's not like that," he lies.

"Well, what's it like, Tom? What exactly do you do for her?"

Shit! he thinks. "I help her. I talk to her. She is a troubled young girl."

"Yes! That's exactly right—she is a *very* young girl."

"Paisley, what's really the matter?"

"What do you mean? I'm just trying to see what you are doing."

"You're not, Paise. There's something else. Just tell me."

"Okay. I just wanted you to feel what I felt the other night, when we made love."

"I did feel it. I loved it. But my mind is everywhere at the moment, even after seeing Simone. It's difficult for me."

"Okay, I understand that. But you know that my feelings for you haven't changed at all. I've tried giving you space, but it's hard when we live together and I can't just touch you!"

"Like I said, my mind is everywhere but in the right frame. Even Simone requested I see her again."

"I knew this was going to happen with Simone! We discussed this before you left her. You said to me, 'Paise, I will leave Simone for you, and I won't ever go back to her. I promise.' I still remember that, Tom. It's something that I will never let go of."

"I know that. I just need some time to think."

"Think about what? I am still in love with you, and I never fell out of love with you. You fell out of love with *me*. And you know when I knew something was wrong? I knew when you told me seventeen months ago that we should sleep in separate rooms, because you needed to focus on your work!"

Her assumption has completely thrown him out, leaving him speechless.

She says, "Can you please come past here so I can show you how I truly feel about you?"

"I know how you feel about me, Paisley. I just can't come past right now." Her sudden lack of speech, combined with the sounds of sniffling, denote that she is not in a good way. Remorsefully, he says, "Paise …"

"No, Tom. I'm so sorry, but I cannot do this anymore. I now know exactly where I stand, and that is completely away from you. I will pack my things and head off to my dad's. I cannot sit here all alone, waiting for you to come home—and when you finally do get home, I don't know where you've been or what you've done. I can't go on like this. It'll completely destroy whatever I have left in my heart."

"Paise …"

"No!" she interrupts. "I never thought that I could ever lose you, Tommy. But I know now that everything in life has a possibility, an outcome. I won't ever get over you. Anyway, I'll let you get back to whatever it is that's more important than me."

A minute after Paisley disconnected the call, Tom storms through their apartment door, forcing it to hit the wall in the house. Stampeding through the home, he tosses an envelope on the table and then spots Paisley dressed in a Chelsea football club guernsey with her black leggings. She attempts to sit over the sofa, but he grabs her bicep.

"Paise!" he barks.

"Who's in the envelope?" she queries.

His head turns towards the table where he tossed the envelope. "Paise, you're not leaving!"

Overlooking his demand, she says, "Is it another client?"

Again he looks over at the table. "Yes, Paise!"

"So you weren't lying that you were at the drop box, then. Have you viewed the profile of the client yet?"

"Not as yet. I wanted to come home so we could look at it together, like we used to do."

"But why were you going to Lancy's?"

With her hand in his, he replies, "Because she messages me and needs me all the time. She has tried twice to kill herself. I have to be there for her, whenever she calls for me."

"Yes, I remember that's how I was when I met you ... I just don't want what happened with you and me to happen with you and her. I'm so afraid of that."

The deceptiveness that Tom has succumbed to is starting to destroy any dignity he has left. However, he knows that now isn't the right time to mention to Paisley the love he feels for Lancy.

"I hate this distance that we have between us. It's as though you are so close to me, but so far away that I can't grab a hold of you. I mean, I don't even know any more if it is your work that is consuming you so much. I even asked Dad to try to go easy on you with the clients, and he claims that he *has* gone easier ... I'm confused, Tom!"

Avoiding eye contact, he focuses on her hand that he is caressing. *I really need to tell her. But how do I tell her? This is going to break me ... I must wait a little longer—I can't reveal this as yet.*

Seeing that Tom isn't reacting to her comments, she is completely aware that something isn't quite right, so she exhales and says, "Tom, I know you, okay? I know that there is something not right with you. You can lie to me and speak whatever excuse you feel you need to, but understand this: if you do not come out with what is really going on, I can no longer be a part of this—a part of you."

"Paisley …"

"Tom, save it. Look, go do whatever it is you have to do. And if you don't tell me the truth by tonight when you get home—in time for dinner—I'm sorry, but I'm out of here. I won't be discussing this topic again."

CHAPTER 52

So Many Messages

With over six messages on his phone, Tom hastily scrolls through them. He discovers that five were from Laney, and one was from Simone. Having a sense that something may be wrong, he decides to read Simone's message first.

"Tom, your son is wondering why you haven't shown up again to discuss this matter you both have."

With a sudden reality check, he realises that he is falling back into the same position he was in, back when his life had first collapsed. At this moment in time, in the midst of this really long five minutes, every thought of Laney has diminished. Paisley disappeared when he walked out of the house. Simone and Josh are floating unattainably in his mind.

Finally, his thoughts clear, and he is open and ready to absorb anything. He takes this opportunity that the universe has granted him to decide on the actions he is going to take. But one thing that does arouse his empty mind is that he is still parked in the garage of his home. He starts the car and heads off to find the place he goes to when he needs time to think.

Five minutes up the road from his home, he pulls the car into the parking bay in front of a quiet reserve. The serene landscape is comprised of hundreds of pine trees that stand over six stories high, acting like a fence around the whole reserve. The lush green grass beneath the trees act as a mattress when lying flat over it. This is his solitude; this is his place where nothing can disrupt his line of thought.

CHAPTER 53

Meditation

With an open mind, he creates a graph, projecting it over the windscreen. The graph consists of these important issues.

Laney	Paisley	Simone and Josh	Clients
I already distinguished that I am in love with Janey. One major concern is her age. The second is I need to tell society that I love her.	Unfortunately, I no longer feel the love I felt for Paisley. I need to confront her and let her know my true feelings.	I need to see Josh ASAP. I need to explain everything to him, everything that I did to his mum.	Have I lost the motivation I had previously to persist in meeting these clients? I feel that these clients are too much for my heart to withstand.

Is this love I feel for Janey the true love I have longed for?

This could be the same love I felt for the other two.

I know it means that I will not be in good books with her father.

Her father is my saviour, my guardian, my best friend.

I once thought I felt true love with Paisley.

Simone is still in love with me after everything I did to her.

I still do somehow sense a connection with Simone.

I am unable to let her go. But I'm not sure as to why I feel this way.

Simone still lingers in my mind. For what reason?

I did once feel true love with Simone.

Josh needs his father; I haven't been there for him.

First was Paisley, and now it's Janey.

Is this a sign that I need to stop?

It's my job, and it's a home for me to live in. But it's something I feel I need to do, to help these lost souls.

CHAPTER 54

The Verdict

"After thirty-six years, I still don't know what true love is. I thought I had found it with Simone, then Paisley, and now Janey. It isn't true love that I am seeking; I am actually seeking a companion who will care for me, stay with me, laugh with me, cry with me, and tell me that I am doing a great job. I want someone who notices me, and me only. I may have found true love in all three girls, but I favour the one who is the right companion for me. And at this point in time, my companion is Janey.

"My clients must be put to rest. I can no longer move on, knowing that I may find another companion whom I will fall in love with and replace the existing one. I may help a lot of people, but it's I who needs help now. If I am to help myself, my job must be the first thing I discard from my life.

"I will create a to-do list in my notes on my phone, and I will check off all the important responsibilities I need to accomplish, starting with the most important.

- Tell Janey that I love her, and I will not ever let her go.
- Tell Josh everything that he needs to know, and that I will be by his side from here on out.
- Tell Brandon I can no longer take on any more clients. I'm done with this job.
- Tell Simone that I love her.
- Tell Paisley that I can no longer be with her, because I've fallen out of love with her.

Oblivious to what he has typed, he is convinced that all is perfect. Now he will start his journey into making amends and recovering whatever he has left in his life.

CHAPTER 55

Tell Janey That I Love Her and Will Not Ever Let Her Go

All five messages Laney had sent him were of no consequence. None were threatening; they were simply playful messages asking where he was. One message that was a photo of herself. Her face is displayed close up as she blows a kiss to him.

His initial response is, "Janey, you are so beautiful. I will see you in about fifteen minutes."

After fourteen minutes, he arrives at the driveway of her home. To his surprise, he is confronted with a vehicle parked at the premises. Thinking it's her mother, he parks on the street and then texts Lancy again, even though she hadn't responded to his earlier message.

"Janey, who's parked in your driveway?" Baffled from a lack of a response from her, he scopes the place thoroughly from inside his vehicle. The curtains are open, but there are silhouettes of people inside. Staring diligently at his phone, his agitation rises due to a lack of response.

"What is she doing?" he mumbles. When he checks his phone again, the chat bubble appears solidly.

Over ten minutes pass, and the chat bubble still remains solid, with no message coming through. His agitation has now shifted to anger that is forcing him to yell out expletives. "Fucking type the message already," he screams, slamming the phone over the dashboard and watching it drop to the floor of the car. Upon gathering it, he brushes the screen to notice the bubble has finally disappeared. In an aggravated state, he speeds off to his next obligation.

CHAPTER 56

Tell Josh Everything That He Needs to Know, and That I Will Be by His Side from Here on Out

His emotions have weakened due to the failure of not being able to fulfil his first obligation. His sense of tranquillity has shifted into agitation, and without any message or phone call, he pulls up into the driveway of Simone's home. He exits the vehicle, completely disregarding his phone. Then at the entrance, he applies three loud thuds to the door.

After several minutes with no answer, he peeks through the window and the crack of the curtain, sensing a vacant home. He applies three strong thuds against the door. Suddenly the door opens to observe Simone dressed in black spandex leggings and a light blue sports singlet. He finds that she is still as beautiful as she was when he first met her. Noticing him peering at her physique, she gives an unwelcoming pose and stands guard at the door.

Tom stutters, "Is Josh in?"

"He is at his friends. He said he'd be back in an hour, about an hour ago."

"Right!"

Not knowing what else to say, she continues. "You should have messaged me, Tom."

"I kind of had a spare moment, and I thought I'd use it wisely."

"You know he is very angry with you."

"I am aware of that, Simone. I just haven't had time. But I'm here now. I'll wait in the car for him."

Shaking her head in disbelief, she adds, "He's met a girl, you know."

"No, I didn't. Is she a girl from school?"

"I'm not sure. I only spoke to her for a minute or so. She is all he speaks about now; He is so happy. He needs you now, Tom, so you and he can talk about her. I'm sure he would love for you to meet her."

With a smile of content, he asks, "So what is she like?"

She responds, "She is a clever young girl. Absolutely beautiful, and she is switched on too. But she seems lost. She seems as though she has something she needs to say but can't quite say it. Anyway, I hope that she likes Josh as much as he likes her. He actually told me he loves her, and I think he really does. The last thing I need is to see his heart get broken. Anyway, I don't want to go on about her anymore—I'm sure Josh wants to tell you."

With such exciting news, finally Tom's frown has turned to a smile.

Sensing his jubilant moment, she says, "You may as well come in."

He sits at the kitchen table, and she routinely prepares a coffee for him. "So how is work going? And how is Paisley?"

His eyebrows raise at the mentioning of Paisley. "Work's fine. I'm actually thinking about quitting and starting a fresh life."

"Oh, okay! Does this fresh life involve Paisley?"

Remaining composed, he responds, "I'm actually not quite sure where I'm heading with Paisley."

Upon hearing those long-awaited words, her eyes light up with a sigh of relief. Incapable of speaking, she tries conjuring up anything to keep the conversation going. Her hand trembles nervously as she digs deep within her wounded mind, searching for some sort of response. She lowers the mug as it almost spills over the rim from her constant tremble. "Um, so … um. I hope it works out for you," she says, exhaling hard and knowing she displayed anxiety within her response.

Aware of her nervousness, he changes the subject. "Hey, I left my phone in the car. Can you message Josh to find out how long he is going to be?"

"Sure," she says, quickly sending him the message. With a stare, she delves deep into his eyes, trying to answer questions she so anxiously needs to ask. With an unexpected brush of confidence, she blurts out, "Tom, can you sense the feelings I have towards you?"

"What do you mean?" he asks.

"Come on, Tom. I have not been with any man since you left me. I saw it in my heart that you would return to me. I felt it, and I waited. My god, did I wait. And don't for one second think that I haven't had any opportunities, cos I have had countless opportunities. But I don't want to go against my heart. I don't want my heart to ache any more than it already has." He breaks the eye contact to stare at the table. "Can you truly sit there, look me dead in the eyes and tell me that you no longer have any feelings for me?" Their eyes make contact. "Go on, please. Just put me out of my misery."

"Janey, I just …"

Instantly her eyebrows raise in shock. Her jaw drops and then closes. "What? Who the hell is Janey, Tom?"

He vigorously shakes his head. "Did I say Janey? Sorry, she is a client of mine, and she has been hassling me for the past two days. Her name is kind of implanted in my mind at the moment." His deceit evades the interrogation—barely.

"Please tell me that she is not a client like Paisley was … Oh, God! It is happening all over again!" She shakes her head.

"No, Simone!" he says, standing his ground. "She is a teenager, for Christ's sake. She just needs professional help …" Abruptly, this conversation sends Tom resilient messages of realism. He is now completely aware that he is blatantly lying to her. He finally assures himself that he doesn't want to do it anymore. Laney's unreturned message, his blatant lies, and all that Simone is confirming to him has raised itself up high on his rage list. He knows that he needs to put a stop to all these lies.

The front door pushes open, and they hear, "Mum?"

"We are in here, Joshy," Simone says, trying to disregard what she suddenly senses.

Upon entering, Josh spots Tom and says, "Dad?" Then he happily embraces him.

Tom thought the worst when he was going to see Josh again, but Josh must feel a sense of relief that Tom is back in his life, so he is happy to show his appreciation. In excitement, Tom asks, "Would you like to join me at a café up the road? I am ready to come clean about everything, Josh. I want you …" He catches Simone's eyes and adds, "Back in my life."

Josh replies, "Yeah, of course. I know a nice one up the road."

"Oh, you do, do ya? Is this where you took your date?"

Josh notices his mother smiling at him and says, "Mum! Did you tell him?"

Simone smiles. "Not everything, sweetie. I saved all the important stuff for you."

Tom watches Josh make his way into his car. While standing by the entrance outside the home, he says to Simone, "I will be back to speak with you maybe tomorrow sometime. Is this okay?"

"Tom, just talk to our son. Guide him as a father would—in the right direction. That is all I want from you, for now."

His arms embrace her, and they finally collide heart to heart. From the pressure of the embrace, Simone yearns so desperately for this, accepting it and seizing every second of it.

CHAPTER 57

You Have a Lot of Messages

Tom enters the vehicle and looks to Josh, who is already in the passenger seat with his seatbelt fastened. Josh stares at the centre console and says, "Dad, your phone was beeping like mad—you have a shit load of messages. It was on the seat, so I put it in the centre console for you."

Tom's eyes turn towards the centre console, and then he responds, "Okay. Did you see who it was from?"

"I didn't try to look, Dad, but I noticed a Janey as I was placing it in the centre console."

"I'm sure its fine. I'm with my son now, so the world can wait."

CHAPTER 58

The Café

Seated by the window, Josh stares diligently at his dad, who is busy ordering the coffee for the both of them. He has a big smile on his face, in relief that he has his father back. Whilst gazing at Tom, Josh's mind gathers any significant info he needs to share that will be of an importance to his father.

Tom is finally seated across from his son, and he admires the smile his Josh expresses. He then kicks off the conversation. "Okay where do I start?"

Josh responds, "Up to you, Dad. I have a lot I need to tell you too. So start where you're comfortable."

"Okay, well, just stop me when you need to question anything. Here I go. Your mother and I met at a very young age. I have to say that it was love at first sight. We were inseparable, and nothing got in our way. No one could change our way of thinking. It was just the two of us that existed in our own little world.

"I'm sure you're already aware that we had you accidently at a very early age in our lives. But the most important thing to the both of us was that we never once thought that we were going to abort you. We were given a chance at life, so why should we take away someone else's chance? We both agreed without any altercation.

"You, Josh, meant the world to the both of us. We gave up all that we ever had interest in, just to make sure that you lived the proper childhood life. But we didn't see it as a loss; we loved every minute that we spent together. It was our unified family. It was all that we ever needed.

"Then work got far too hectic. My business was driving me insane. My relief was when I got home to be with you and your mum. I hated feeling that way, and I knew life wasn't meant to be a stressful one, but I did nothing about it. I started to get depressed, and your mum noticed the signs. She tried her hardest to help me, but she knew there was no helping me—not in this business. My depression worsened day by day, and I always took out my anger on your mother. I'm so sorry I'm telling you this."

Josh replies, "It's fine, Dad. Just go on."

"Okay, so one day, I got home from work. I yelled so profoundly and demonically at your mother. But your mother always stood by me, and I knew from there that I needed to seek help. I then met this man—a hero in my eyes—who had miraculously managed to help me, to save me. I'm not sure how, but he did it. He stopped me from killing myself just with his words, his persistence. Yes, Josh, I had reached the stage where I was done with life, and I chose to kill myself. Anyway, this man helped me to a point where we became great friends, and we saw so much of each other."

"The first thing he made me do was quit my job, my business. Believing in him the way I did, I succumbed to his demands. As time went by, your mum was working, thankfully, and she helped out a lot. But we both knew I needed to get a job—a job that I'm good at, a job that I can thrive on, a job at which I can express my true talents.

"Well, this close friend of mine has a daughter who was in the same boat as I have been. She was younger than me, and she was into very bad drugs and living a dreadful life. When I met his daughter by accident at his home, she turned up wanting money, so we kicked out the entourage she had with her, and we sat her down on the sofa to talk to her. We found out on that day that I had the touch to help people who are in need of help. Her father was unable to help her because she never gave him the opportunity to help her. In return, as a favour to my friend, I helped his daughter get her life back in order. And he will thank me as much as I will thank him for the rest of our lives."

"Is this that girl mum always bad-mouths?"

"Yes, Josh, it is. It's Paisley. Anyway, Paisley and I had obliviously fallen for each other. Whilst helping her, I felt that I was losing time that needed to be spent with your mother, and it led me to seek a companion, someone who devoted her time to me. Even though your mother always did that, I lost everything I felt for her once I fell for Paisley. As soon as I committed adultery on your mother, I knew it was time to leave her be and let her move on with her life. It killed me to see her face, but I didn't feel the same connection we felt when we met. It was Paisley who had completely occupied my mind.

"So anyway, my new job consisted of helping people whom my friend was unable to help. He works for a lifeline company that helps people who are in need, but what he witnessed throughout his life was the loss of so many souls that were untreatable. It killed him to see that happening, so he gave the clients he couldn't help to me, and I try my best to talk to them and steer them into the right direction."

Josh intervenes. "Wait! Is this the same lifeline company I called for myself? Is your friend's name Patrick?"

With a smirk, Tom responds, "That is the friend I'm speaking of, yes. But his name isn't Patrick. He isn't allowed to reveal his true identity, because the people he tries to help could blame him and try to search for him, if they felt they needed to seek revenge on him."

"Oh, right! That makes sense. So wait a minute! What happens to the people you are unable to help?"

"Well …"

Josh's phone rings, interrupting the story. Josh removes his phone and answers it with an expressive smile.

CHAPTER 59

An Interruption

"Hey, you. How are you?" Josh says while standing up and walking outside. "Are you okay? I was thinking about you."

"I'm fine, Josh. I just have a lot on my plate at the moment. I'm actually wondering what you're doing right now."

"Really? You want to meet up?"

"I don't know … What are you doing? Are you busy?"

"I'm actually with my dad. Can you believe it? He just popped up at Mum's house and brought me to the café you and I went to."

"Oh, that's so sweet …" she says, relieved to know of Tom's whereabouts.

"You want to come here and meet him? I would love you to."

In complete shock, she loses her words before responding, "Nah, I'd better not;"

"Why not? Come on. He would love you."

"I'm sure he will … But I'd better not, Josh. How about I see you tomorrow, or whenever you can?"

"No, I want you to come here. For starters, I've missed the shit out of you. You've already met my mum, so it's only fair that you meet Dad, don't you think? And … I think they may have seemed to have found a connection again."

"Really? What makes you say this?"

"They embraced one another before Dad and I had left."

"Oh, that's nice!" she lies in frustration. "I'm actually really tired, though."

"You can't be, Laney. You just asked me what I was doing. Are you embarrassed to meet him or something?"

"No, of course not …"

"Well, come on, then. I'll buy you a coffee. Please?" he begs.

"Okay, but I'm telling you now that your father may not like it."

"Like what, Laney? That you may be my girlfriend?"

She shrugs. "Well, yes, I suppose."

"What's not to like about a beautiful girl like you? You know what? I won't even tell him you're coming. I'll surprise him."

She stands her ground and says, "No. I think you should tell him, Josh"

"Nah, he'll be fine, I'm sure. How long do you think before you get here?"

She halts suddenly, squeezing her head and trying to relieve the pressure she feels in her mind. She then shakes her head vigorously, reassuring herself that it's not a good idea to meet in a surprise. "I'd better not, Josh. I feel out of place. This is supposed to be for the two of you."

"No!" he screams with angst. "You're coming. I need to see you."

Sensing a miffed sound in his voice, she replies, "Okay, okay. I am about ten minutes away."

"Awesome! I can't wait to see you again, Lancy."

She's momentarily unresponsive. Finally, she finds her words and says, "Yeah, me too. I'll see you soon …"

Upon disconnecting the call with Josh, she types a message to Tom, trying to warn him of her sudden invitation.

CHAPTER 60

The Café, Scene Two

"Who was that on the phone?" Tom asks.

"Oh, it was just a friend. Sorry. Please continue."

"Right! I was pretty much wrapping it up before you received the phone call." While gazing at the ceiling, he delves into his mind, trying to recall where he left off. "Oh, yes. So that's my job description now. I found I was happy to do this job, until my most recent cases. Now I feel I'm done with it."

"So what will you do?"

"Well, I'm not quite sure. I am leaving my options open."

"So, you and Paisley? Are you still in love?"

Smiling in shame, he responds, "We were once, but it's been a little rocky at the moment."

With excitement Josh responds, "So does this mean you will go back to Mum?"

Tom's eyebrows raise. "Well, I'm not sure yet …"

CHAPTER 61

Laney

After having sent endless text messages to Tom that haven't been responded to, she reduces her pace, frightened to face the love of her life as he has to watch her hold the hand of his son. From the corner of the street, where she can perceive the café, she halts momentarily. *Why isn't he bloody replying?*

CHAPTER 62

An Unexpected Scene

While savouring every sip of his coffee, finally Josh peers through the window, spotting Laney approaching the café. Noting his son's excitement, Tom smiles and then turns towards the window to unexpectedly find Laney standing there, waving at Josh.

Immediately time seizes. Tom's heart sinks to the base of his chest, causing severe pains that come across as a heart attack. The early morning image of the text message he spied on Laney's phone answered his question about who Josh is. The pain worsens to a point where the only relief is when he presses his hand against his heart. His breathing is scarce; sweat instantly appears on his forehead, dripping down his nose. The deep breaths aren't helping him at all, and Laney hasn't even entered the café yet.

Josh is out there touching her, placing his hands all over her frail body, happily conversing with her. His sweaty palm rests over the serviette, gluing the serviette to it as he lifts it off the table. He looks to the drenched serviette and then wipes the constant flow of sweat from off his brow. The relentless pain in his chest fails to ease, and his heart thumps at a pace where he feels as though it'll break through his bones and out of his skin, landing on the table in front of him. Helplessly, he watches them enter into the café.

"Dad, this beautiful girl is Laney." She stands before him, looking down at Josh's hand resting around her waist.

Instantly, Tom's eyes fall to the table in remorse. Laney's face appears pale, and she feels mortified, as if she has cheated on Tom, even though she has done nothing but converse with Josh. Her shameful expression displays her remorse towards her lover, acknowledging that this is destroying her as much as it destroys Tom.

"Dad, are you okay? You don't look so good. You appear as though you've seen a ghost!"

Unresponsive, Tom thinks for a moment to be sure he remains adult about this situation. He apprehensively raises his sweaty palm, offering it to Laney. She extends a shaking hand to meet his.

"It's nice to meet you," he says, glancing away from her eyes. He then refocuses on Josh and says, "Josh, I need to head off, so I'll leave you two be. Just call me whenever you like." Laney shamefully holds her gaze at her feet until Josh ominously says, "Dad, what's wrong? Are you okay?"

"I think I must be coming down with something, son. Just have fun. I'm fine. I'll talk to you later." As he walks away, he doesn't lay an eye on Laney.

Abruptly, Laney releases the grasp Josh held over her. Then she hastily runs to the bathroom of the café.

To her surprise, she finds the bathroom empty, and she locks the door behind her. She turns the faucet to its maximum turn and then watches the steam from the hot water float up into the air, creating an instant haze over the mirror. In angst, she pounds her hand against the mirror, marking the haze. She roughly clears the haze in the shape of a rainbow, finally revealing the disloyalty of her face. Unexpectedly, she hears a loud thud against the door, disrupting her gaze. She crudely demands, "Sorry—it's occupied."

Josh says, "Laney, it's me. Are you okay?"

Shit, I bloody forgot about Josh. Fuck! Wiping her tears, she says, "I'm fine, Josh. I just felt a little under the weather. Can you please give me five minutes?"

"I hope you're okay! I'll be here waiting for you."

Her eyes begin to bawl. It is so severe that she is unable to control the sobs that escape. She knows she has tainted the love that she and Tom created together. She knows that she should've come out with the truth when she was asked the question.

Her disgraceful appearance finally appears in the hazy mirror, displaying a sight of her that she's dreaded to ever perceive. Her heart believed, that the next time she perceived herself through a mirror, it would've been on a joyous occasion. Through the satanic image she gazes at, her voice deepens as she says, "You're a fucking slut, Janey Lane!"

CHAPTER 63

Take Me Away

Tom's vehicle moves at a speed of over 110 kilometres down an endless freeway. The frequent signage on the side of road has been completely disregarded. While staring at the open road, his appearance is of a demonic state. His phone is on standby on the floor, in the back of the vehicle. Images clutter his mind—images of his beloved Laney kissing Josh on the lips. He pounds the steering wheel several times, trying to focus on the music he's blaring. The music is just noise in the background, and his mind continues to create different scenes of sexual conduct involving Laney and his son.

A flashing light on the dashboard beeps loudly, to jolt him back to reality. His eyes veer toward the flashing light only to realise his fuel is almost at empty. His focus suddenly regains, and he must find a petrol station as soon as he can.

Twenty kilometres up the road, he spots a station that looks to be deserted. He pulls into the station, scoping the shop front to see if the place is indeed vacant. Fortunately, he spots a man standing in the shop, allowing him access to pump petrol.

CHAPTER 64

The People He Left Behind

Laney	Josh and Simone	Paisley
I don't get it. I've sent him over ten messages, and I've called him, but the phone doesn't even ring.	"Why won't he answer my calls, why is his phone off?"	"Dad, he won't answer my calls. His phone is off."
This is all my fault.	"It's okay, Josh. He does this when he needs his time out."	"Maybe he is with his son?"
I caused this.	"But, Mum, he always answers his phone and messages. I'm actually scared now. Maybe we should ask Paisley? Do you think he is with her?"	"No, Dad. It's been three days now. I'm scared."
What am I going to do?		"It does sound weird. Did he get the new client I left him four days ago?"
I've gotta try to contact Josh, even though I haven't heard from him since that day I left the café.		

He probably won't even answer me, and he will question as to why the hell I am curious about his dad.

What do I do? Do I speak to Mum? But Mum will hate me for everything I've done and most likely have caused.

Adam, I need you now. Give me a sign that Tom is okay. Please, Adam, I beg you. I'm really afraid about this.

"I am not ever going to contact Paisley, Josh. I'm sorry, honey. I just can't do it."

"Well, where could he be?"

"Josh, he is a big boy. I'm sure he is okay."

"Mum, we have to do something. I'm so afraid that something has happened to him."

"Yeah, it's here right in front of me, opened, but he never read it. I think I might call Simone. Or do you want to call Simone?"

"Honey, I don't want to call Simone. She will be upset if I do."

"Please, Dad. I'm desperate. I can't just sit here and let this go. I love him. I'm so afraid right now."

CHAPTER 65

Found a Room

Confined in a five-metre by five-metre room and stretched out over his bed, he notices the tiny bathroom to the right of him and a non-functional TV hung lopsided over the wallpapered wall. Completely unaware of where he is, he shuts his eyes whilst stretching his arms and legs, making up for the hours he had them bent in the vehicle.

His phone rests unattainable on the floor in the vehicle. The world he left behind is suddenly of no interest to him. His exhaustion is sending delusional thoughts throughout his mind. He has convinced himself that he was the cause of Laney seeking an interest in Josh. He is completely aware that he betrayed Paisley, Simone, and Josh, he and knows that he has scarred the people he loves.

His eyelids become heavy, to the point where he can no longer withstand the stress. It isn't long before he finally succumbs. Moments later, he is away in dream land.

CHAPTER 66

Laney

$\mathcal{L}$aney stares up at the ceiling from her bed. The awaited sign from Adam hasn't come through at all. Having absolutely nobody to turn to, she tries to sort out matters herself but finds that she fails every time. With the constant glimpses of her phone awaiting something from Tom, she realises the time is 2:34 a.m. The date underneath the time makes her realise that it has been six days now. The heaviness within her teary eyes inevitably forces them shut.

After several hours, she wakes to a fright, sensing an energy hovering over the top of her. The energy feels deep, as though it caresses her upper torso. The unnerving energy feels warm over the parts where it hovers, but everywhere else is unbearably cold. This unsuspected energy frightens her to a point where she is unable to move. Finding strength in her arms, she stretches to grasp her phone, trying to recall the date she had witnessed earlier. After a quick calculation in her mind, she announces, "Shit! It didn't come …"

CHAPTER 67

Police Involved

"Yes, Officer. Well, it's been about seven days now. This is unlike him."

"Miss Wethers, have you tried contacting your husband?"

"Yes, of course I have! I told you I have, many times. His phone is off because it goes straight to his message bank."

"Right, right. Can you hold for a moment?"

"Sure," she says.

Minutes later, the officer asks, "Ma'am, can I have your name, please?"

"My name is Simone Wethers."

"Right! And you are the wife of Mr Wethers. Is this correct?"

"Well, I am, but we separated years ago."

"Right, well that explains a lot, then. Miss Wethers, we received a call a day ago that was exactly the same as yours, fitting your exact description—from another individual."

"Can I ask who it is?"

"Actually, you cannot, but the stories are identical."

"Was it Paisley?"

The officer halts. "I'm truly sorry, ma'am. We are unable to give out any information."

"Right! You know what? Who cares! Just find my husband."

CHAPTER 68

Heading Home

*A*fter a peaceful night's rest away from his chaotic world, his chosen destination is to return back to his home town, finally his heart has made the decision he has been yearning for. Throughout the journey, he will ponder on how he is to confront all who are important to him.

Upon having almost reached his suburb, his phone suddenly appears in his mind. He searches blindly on the floor in the back of the vehicle, touching the rim of the phone with the tip of his index finger. Through strenuous stretching, he fails to realise his car is drifting in and out of the lanes as he stubbornly persists after the phone. A vehicle in the distance rapidly approaches on the opposite side of the road, but he is far too distracted to notice it. After finally grasping his phone and almost dislocating his arm, the vehicle that he fails to spot has swerved metres in front of him, aggressively beeping its horn.

He finally arrives at his place of sanctuary, and he pulls to the curb and parks the car, eagerly wanting to tend to his phone. Upon loading it, messages and missed phone calls flood the screen, taking up several pages. The latest message sent is from Laney. He starts his car again, ignoring every other notification and listening to his heart. Then he heads to his chosen destination.

CHAPTER 69

She Wasn't Home

After several minutes of frequent knocks at the door, there is no response from the house. While staring at his vehicle in the driveway, he ponders what to do next. His initial thought is of Laney and Josh. Vigorously shaking his head, he discards the memory of the day at the café, trying to remain focused. "Think, Tom! Think!" he says, squeezing his head with his hands. His eyes suddenly open wide with gratitude as he says, "I've got it! I know where she is."

CHAPTER 70

Laney

After pulling into the curb at the park, he glances at the tree whilst he parks his vehicle. The Adam and Eve tree looks vacant and undisturbed. He refuses to believe it, because he trusts his gut feeling.

He runs towards the tree. As he reaches it, she is nowhere to be seen. Suddenly he drops to his knees and looks to the sky, screaming out from the top of his lungs. "Laney!" His head drops in disappointment as his eyes close, trying to hold back his tears.

"Laney," he says in an apologetic manner.

Seconds later, an angel's voice appears—a voice he has longed for, a voice he fell in love with, a voice that manages to ignite his heart. The soft voice calls, "Tom-Tom?" His head jerks up, searching for his angel. Finally, she reveals herself from behind the tree. Without wasting another moment, they run to each other. Laney leaps up, landing in Tom's arms. He embraces her, holding her tight. They remain connected, refusing to let one another go. The world around them has disappeared, and time stands still for them. Neither of them has ever experienced anything like this before; they are both aware that this is true love. He kisses her tear-sodden lips as if eagerly eating at the succulence they are currently producing. The taste of her tears offers him a sense of comfort.

Once reality steps in, she pulls away from Tom's lips and stares at his face. "Baby, I missed you. You scared the hell out of me," she says whilst pecking at his lips.

Unable to control his tears, he happily sheds them, knowing he is safe to be himself in front of his true love.

"Hey, hey. Stop crying. You are safe now. We are finally together, my Tom-Tom."

His cries suddenly become far more convincing. He sets her down, and she taps his back comfortingly.

"Shh, shh. It's okay, baby. I'm here. Hey, look at me," she demands with her finger under his chin. "Did you see my message?"

Glancing into her eyes, he shakes his head.

"Well, can you please read it for me?" Lost for words, he fails to respond to her. "Where is your phone, baby?" she asks, searching his pockets.

It's tucked in his back pocket. She removes it to take full control of it whilst his head rests on her shoulder. Peering at the screen, she unexpectedly stumbles across the last message he's received, which is from Paisley. Irately, she swipes to read it.

"Hey, Tommy. I need to tell you something. I don't know if you will ever come back, or what has happened with you, but I just want you to know that I think I'm pregnant." Her eyes open wide in shock. "I didn't get my period. I know I am unable to procreate, but I have a strong feeling this time … Please, when you see this, I need to talk to you." A flood of tears flow out of Laney's eyes. She doesn't want Tom to know she is crying, so she tries to stay strong, containing herself the best she can. After finally pulling through, she settles on swiping the message, eradicating it.

She then opens her message and says, "Tom, look at the phone, baby." He moves his head, wiping the flood of tears from his eyes. He pulls her hand in toward him and then reads it.

"Hey, Tom. I didn't get my period, so I took a pregnancy test and found that it was positive. I'm pregnant with your baby, Tom …"

CHAPTER 71

Time Stops for Tom

As soon as Tom acknowledges the word *pregnant*, his heart skips a beat, and time stops again. His eyes open wide with joy but at the same time fear. Joy from impregnating the person he loves dearly; fear from the judgemental world around him—a world that doesn't accept this sort of behaviour; a world where mistakes like these are inexcusable. This world will not let Tom accept this gift and cherish it in his lasting years. This beautiful girl, this new-found love he wasn't searching for, this companion who has miraculously fallen into his lap stands tranquil in front of him. She is far too young to understand. She is the most beautiful girl he has ever laid his eyes on, so beautiful and innocent that she is completely unaware of what this world is capable of.

He feels depleted and knows he cannot celebrate this news. He doesn't know how he can express his emotions to the girl he loves. She deserves the best of everything. She deserves the best life her angels can offer her. Are they enough, though? The angels that look down on her and keep her happy and protected from the evils of this world—are these angels enough? Do they have the power they need to protect her? *I will be sure to summon these angels and do what I need to do, to keep her happy. I will stay happy and keep my character going until it's the right time to switch it off.*

CHAPTER 72

Back in Real Time

$\mathcal{T}$om thinks, *I need to show her that I am ecstatic. I need for her to believe me.*

Finally, he notices her deep gaze into his eyes, and she says, "There you are. You left me for a good two minutes. Are you okay?" She shakes her head and adds, "Anyway, what do you think?" She is anxious.

He looks at her with a smile. "You want to know what I think?" She nods her head in a cute manner. "I am over the moon!" He announces whilst picking her up off her feet to hold her in his arms.

She holds her hand at his chest, rejecting the embrace. Then she says, "Are you serious, Tom? I'm sorry—I just don't feel that."

Standing idle, he expresses a smile that reveals dishonesty within his heart. "But why don't you believe it?"

"Well …" She taps the soil on the base of the tree. "Sit!" Abiding her request, he sits beside her. "There are many reasons as to why I'm not quite feeling it. The first is you can't act for shit! Second, I thought you would've gotten so angry with me, because I totally forgot to buy the morning-after pill. You need to believe me on that, Tom: I really did forget. Third was that you saw me with Josh, and I thought that would've completely destroyed you."

He retorts, "Laney, listen to me!"

With her palm to his face, she interrupts him. "See, you are calling me Laney. You always called me …"

He persists. "Jancy, listen to me now. In this life, all I ever want is for you to tell me the truth, if you are to be my girl. I no longer care about society and its judgemental ways. I will be the best I can be. I will be here every step of the way."

With an expression that reveals her true feelings, her feelings of knowing she is loved by the person she is madly in love with, her heart suddenly intervenes, controlling her vocal chords. "Tom, wait! I need to tell you something."

He looks to her, fearing the worst as he takes deep breaths of air. "What is it, Jancy?"

She exhales soft and slow and then says, "Tom, when I was trying to bring up the message I sent to you on your phone, there was one that was sent after mine. It was from Paisley."

"Yes, and?"

"Well, I deleted it …"

"Why would you do that? Well, what did it say?"

"Because I want you all to myself …"

"Jancy, that isn't fair."

"I know, Tom, I know. Please don't be mad."

"It's fine, Jancy. So what did it say?"

"Well, she said that she thinks she is pregnant."

Furious, he jumps to his feet as though he witnessed a massive spider crawling in front of him. "What gave you the right to look at my message, Jancy?"

Instantly, she bursts into tears. "No, Tom. What gives you the right to sleep with whomever you feel like?"

"Janey, I slept with Paisley before you! My mind is flooded with mixed feelings. Paisley and I hadn't had sex or been intimate for a very long time, and she threw herself onto me. Even though my feelings for you were so strong, it was a way for me to try to convince myself that I can't be in love with someone so young. I thought it would've changed my feelings, but it never did! I'm madly in love with you."

Remorsefully, she adds, "Tom, I don't even care that you slept with Paisley. I kind of had the feeling you did, but the universe helped me discard that out of my mind." She looks to the heavens whilst pressing her palms together. "What I *do* care about is why you would try to convince yourself that you don't love someone, regardless of her age. Not many people get to experience true love, and we both did. You should've accepted it as a gift from the universe. I did ask the universe if I could experience true love, and I thought it would've been with Jacob. Instead, it was you. They heard my plea, and they didn't want to give me Jacob because they had you, ready and waiting. I wasn't even 100 per cent sure as to whom it would be with, but the universe knew all along."

Acknowledging every word she speaks, his mind is tossing images of Paisley holding a baby. He shakes his head and says, "Janey, I'm truly sorry, but I must go to Paisley right now."

"But you said you love me."

"Janey, listen. I love you with all my heart, and I will never stop loving you. I know we conquered true love, because none has ever felt as it does with you."

She starts to cry uncontrollably and moves into him,

hoping he accepts her embrace. He accepts with open arms, holding her to his chest. She then pulls her head away from his chest to look up to him. He looks down into her teary eyes, wipes the trail of tears from her cheek with his thumb, and moves in to kiss her.

It is that moment where, just by a simple kiss, a simple tick of silence manages to express so many unspoken words to one another. This one moment, this one kiss they yearned for, is so compelling, so extraordinary, so understanding. Both acknowledging, while Lancy sensing within her heart, that this may well be her very last kiss, knowing that he may choose to pursue a life with Paisley Upon sensing this, she moves her face away from his and presses her head against his chest to quietly sob at the future she foresees.

"Tom," she says with a croaky voice, "Thank you for blessing me with this gift that is inside me."

He drops his head, bawling uncontrollably. After wiping the flood of tears, he retorts, "Janey, I'm so sorry, but I must go …"

She cries hysterically, grabbing hold of his wrists.

He adds, "Janey, I loved you at the tree, and I will love you forever in me." He shrugs off the tight grasp she has, kissing the roof of her hands. While her head is bowed down, he uses that moment to walk away.

She drops to her knees, wailing. Finally, her head flicks upward to watch her lover casually walk away from her.

CHAPTER 73

Paisley

Upon opening the garage door, Tom finds Paisley's vehicle still parked inside. He storms into the house, desperately searching for her, and he finds her lying almost naked over his bed. Used tissues are scattered all over the bed and the floor. He grabs her by the bicep, turning her around. Her make-up is smeared all over her tear-streaked face. At the very sight of him, she continues her sobbing, and then she accepts the embrace he offers to her.

"Shh, I'm here now, Paise."

That one whisper drives her to bawl more aggressively. "Tommy, I'm pregnant!" she says, hoping for an extended embrace.

"I know, Paisley. I saw your message." he says. "I'm so happy that you finally fell pregnant."

"We, Tom. *We* fell pregnant. God finally answered my prayers."

"He did!" he affirms.

With the blanket covering them, they lay peacefully until Paisley's eyes finally close. Upon reaching her long-awaited slumber, he heads out of the bedroom to gather three pieces of paper. He seats himself on the desk in the study area of the home, prepping his black calligraphy pen for an hour's worth of writing.

What he thought was going to take an hour, actually takes several. Finally, he proofreads and edits all he wrote to his exact liking. He then places the three letters in three different envelopes, and then he writes something over the front of each of them.

The envelope that has Paisley's name written over the front of it, is placed neatly on the kitchen table, in the family room of their home. After having one last look at his place of rest, he smiles and then heads to his car.

CHAPTER 74

The Tom-Tom and Laney Tree

This popular public park houses an abundance of children who callously abuse the playground, whilst their mothers are busy taking selfies to upload onto social media. Ignoring the disobedience around the park, he heads straight to the Adam and Eve tree.

Behind the area of the vast tree where Laney sometimes hid, he notices a fresh engraving on it. Engraved in capital letters, it reads, "Tom-Tom and Laney's tree." Underneath that perfect engraving is another message that reads, "The place where the miracle of true love was born."

He bows his head, and sulks momentarily whilst gazing at the tree in search of a hole of some sort. To his surprise, near the base of the trunk, he finds the perfect hole. Then he looks to the heavens and says, "Thank you!"

In the inner pocket of his jacket, he removes the envelope with Janey Lane's name written over it. Then he rolls the envelope to fit it into the hole. After one last scan of the vast tree, he nods several times in understanding of the importance of this gift of nature. Then he walks away from where it began.

CHAPTER 75

Simone Wasn't at Home

Trying to be as conspicuous as he can, Tom parks his vehicle on the street across from Simone's home. With no vehicle in the driveway, the house seems to be locked up for the night. His jacket's inner pocket houses the final envelope, which he discreetly inserts into the letterbox. He hastily heads back to his car, speeding off to his next destination.

CHAPTER 76

His Refuge

The sun shines ever so brightly on such a peaceful day. From in his vehicle, he gazes at a certain ray of sunshine, pinpointing a designated zone that seems perfect for the place of his refuge. He opens the boot of his car to gather the infamous black, unopened briefcase. Beside the case, he takes a picnic blanket and then heads toward the refuge zone.

Thankfully, at this present time, the landscape is entirely unoccupied, apart from the chirping rainbow lorikeets singing their gratifying song to the heavens.

While seated comfortably over the blanket, he rests both palms over the briefcase as though he is attempting some sort of a healing procedure. In a meditative state, he administers a soothing breathing pattern to help keep him calm. His eyes open wide as he turns the dial of the six combination locks to their correct numbers.

As the latches raise, he uses the tip of his thumbnails to fit inside the tiny crack of the opening. He raises the lid of the brief case, watching it fold back to its farthest position.

Inside the mysterious case sits a neatly placed large syringe, accompanied with three sealed liquid-filled tubes.

On the far-right side of the briefcase is a tourniquet. He carefully opens each bottle, dispensing an exact amount of each liquid from each bottle into the syringe. With the three liquids combined, the syringe is at its full capacity. After tightening the tourniquet, he gazes at the protrusion of his veins. Then without any hesitation, he slowly injects the concoction into his blood vessels.

Once the items are placed correctly back into the case, he locks it up, positioning the case to act as a pillow under his head. While staring up at the blue sky, he removes his phone from his pocket and clicks on the message app to type several messages for three different people.

After the three messages are sent, he switches his phone off for the last time and then places it into his jacket pocket. Relishing the comfort he is currently experiencing, his arms drop by the side of his body as his eyes begin to feel droopy. The glare that glimmers off the strength of the sun shines brightly over his face, forcing his eyes to squint to the point where full closure is the only form of relief.

Only moments after his eyelids had shut, in the far distance, he perceives a white light so bright that it lures him into it. He feels the light calling upon him, dragging him in, and promising him endless love. He walks with his hand ahead of him, trying not to let the brightness blind his vision. But as he moves in closer to the light, the brightness dims to a point where he finds a large gate that is so tall he is unable to distinguish the top of it. He smiles with gratitude, knowing that his long-awaited peace has finally been bestowed upon him.

With all he has left in his vocal chords, he loudly announces, "I'm finally free!"

CHAPTER 77

Simone and Josh's Letter

$\mathcal{A}$ letter rests on the table in front of her, labelled with her and her son's names, awaiting an opening. Ignoring it, she replies again to Tom's text that she received over ten minutes ago. She impatiently taps the tip of her fingernail against the screen with aggravation as she stares deeply at the letter, refusing to open it. In a sudden act of anguish, she lands the base of her fist against the phone, giving in to reading the letter.

Dearest Simone and Josh,

When you read this, I will have already departed from this earth.

Simone, we fell in love with each other because we were supposed to. It was meant to be; it was written for us in the clouds. Through our love, we created Josh. Josh gave us so much strength, so much joy, so much happiness. He was our gift that we treasured all to ourselves.

Through life's hurdles, I lost the love we were once united with; to this day, it haunts me. I couldn't understand why I lost it. I never asked to lose it, and God knows that all I ever wanted was you. I asked myself every day and every night, "Why, God? Why did you take my feeling of love away from my beloved Simone?" He responded to me.

There are many things in life that have explanations, but there is an abundance of things that cannot be explained. Unfortunately, we were one of those abundances.

I'm leaving now, Simone, because I know that my heart has finally retired. It can no longer withstand any more abuse.

Know that I always loved you, Simone, but I was no longer capable of expressing it.

Josh,

Son, don't be the person I became. In life, there is only the one chance. Use that one chance, follow the dream that you have, and follow where your heart wants to take you. Because your heart is the last command that your mind will speak. Always believe your heart and never once doubt it, and please always do as it says. It's always right.

Understand that I feel I don't deserve you in any way. I left your beautiful mother to raise you on her own, and just so you know, I trusted her with all my heart. And look at the fine job she did.

Laney seemed like a beautiful girl. Chase her, Josh. Do right by her, and never give up on her. Go to her when your heart tells you to. I feel it in my heart, the power that this Laney embraces.

I want both of you to never hold something unforgivable in your hearts. You always need to forgive and forget. Don't let anything consume you when it is unneeded. I love you both with all my heart. Please forgive me for all the wrongs I did.

Remember that a change of heart is always the right cure for any negative thought.

Love,

Tom Wethers

CHAPTER 78

Paisley's Letter

$\mathcal{U}$pon entering a vacant room, the first thing Paisley's eyes distinguish is the letter resting on the dinner table. She shakes her head as she reads her name, printed neatly over the front of it. Then she casually opens it up.

Dearest Paisley,

> *When you read this, I will have already departed from this earth.*
>
> *Paisley, we were once privileged enough to have fallen in love. You saw it in your heart that it was all true. I too felt the love that was bestowed upon us. Even though I was aware of your concerns in regards to procreation being a bother for you, it was never a bother for me. I accepted that it was what it was.*
>
> *Indeed, God has answered your prayers, Paisley. He has given you the gift you were longing for. You must cherish this gift and be sure to do everything in your power to guide this gift in the right direction.*
>
> *Know that I will always watch over you, to help guide you and this child in the right direction.*

Move on with your life, Paisley. Find the right soul with whom your heart will unite. Don't think any less of yourself. You are as beautiful as you see yourself. Listen to your heart, because your heart doesn't lie.

Remember that a change of heart is always the right cure for any negative thought.

Oh, one more thing. Please tell your father he was the best person I have ever met, a true friend. Please tell him I finally succumbed to the powers of the briefcase that held the cure for this disease with which I diagnosed myself.

Love,

Tom Wethers

CHAPTER 79

Laney

Laney is seated at her dressing table, staring at her phone, trying to succumb to the text message from Tom. "Janey, head to the Adam and Eve tree. Once you're there, you will find my heart is enclosed in an envelope at the base of the trunk, where you chose to hide from me. I love you, Janey." Without wasting any time, she heads to the tree.

Upon arrival, she ignores society's actions around her. She sprints to the tree, realising she can no longer wait to see this envelope. Within two minutes, she makes her way around the back of the tree. She looks down at the base of the trunk to find a red picnic blanket folded neatly over the floor, and an envelope rolled up and placed neatly in the hole of the trunk. Silently she mouths "Janey Lane," which is written neatly over the front of the envelope.

My beautiful Janey Lane,

Before I begin, I bought this red picnic blanket for you, because I know you would've stormed out of your home and forgotten it.

Janey, you are my true companion, and most important my true love. If this was a film, I would pack all your treasured belongings, and I would fly you to a place where you and I can be free from everything, from everyone, from this dreaded society of judges. But this is not a film. Unfortunately, this is the hardship of life; this is a place where our true love just doesn't fit in.

Our love began at this one tree. This tree had our names written on it without our consent. It was written for us, and we just needed to find it. And we did. I wanted you to come here because I felt in my heart that this was where the universe wanted our hearts to speak to one another. I know that you will always love me, and I know that you will never want another man again. But you need to keep going. Life is already too hard. You cannot spend the rest of yours chasing a ghost. You will meet the one soul who is going to free your mind of the true love you felt for me. You will never feel this love again, but you will feel safe, and you will always know that I am there with you.

If you are to cross paths with Josh again, you must remind him that forgetting the wrongs in life, and forgiving the ones who need it, will extend his life. You cannot hold onto anger, and neither can you choose to not forgive—it will consume you in a way where your life is controlled by society's mistaken accomplishments.

Janey, I will leave you with this line that only you will understand, but in the future you will be able to make many recognize it.

"True love wasn't ever meant to be accomplished on this earth; it is simply a transient of time."

Janey, nobody knows about our true love. I have kept it with me. It is your choice whether you choose to hold it inside you or share it with whomever you choose. Never forget, and never feel the need to have to tell anyone anything about your business. If secrets are far too hard to release to loved ones, the universe will guide you and help you speak what you need to say. Even if it means you may suffer for it.

I need for you to remember always that no matter how you feel, and no matter what is hurting your heart, I will be there, and I will embrace you and help you get through it. You will know I am there with you. You will feel the cold shiver through your bones as I embrace you.

Janey, I love you. I'll be waiting for you.

You will find my shell at my place of sanctuary.

Love,

Your one and only, Tom-Tom Wethers

CHAPTER 80

Six Months Later

$\mathcal{L}$ying helpless in a hospital bed, she awaits the results from her doctor. Her mind is only focused on one thing, and that one thing isn't allowing her to think of anything else. After what feels like five hours, the doctor walks into the room with his binder of files.

"I'm so sorry to tell you this news, Miss Ramone, but the umbilical cord strangled your baby from inside your womb. There was nothing we could do ..."

CHAPTER 81

Notice The Signs

"Kids, move it. We are already late. Joel, grab your sister's bag. Claire, you go in, and I'll see you backstage."

Backstage was a disaster. Claire awaits orders from her teacher whilst the make-up artists paint her face. The instructor spots Claire's mother and says, "Hello, Miss Lane."

Gasping for air, Miss Lane responds, "Hey, Sophie. Sorry we are late. These kids are so laid back. Nothing fazes them whatsoever.

"That's completely fine. Please don't stress. Claire is the lead dancer, and she is expected to be here before the others, but you're not late, so it's fine."

Smiling at the consideration, Claire announces, "Mummy, I'm scared to do this!"

Before she is able to respond, she has a sudden sense of coldness embracing the entirety of her torso. She shivers from the embrace and then confidently responds, "Sweetie, Daddy is with us right now. I can feel his presence, and he says you'll be great. Make him proud, Claire."

With a sense of relief, Claire smiles and then heads onto stage with confidence.

Sophie claps her hands and then looks to Miss Lane and says, "She'll be fine, Miss Lane. She is a natural."

She smiles back at her then responds, "Thank you so much, Sophie. But please, call me Laney …"

That's all I've got—for now …
Thank you!

ABOUT THE AUTHOR

Adrian De Nittis was born in Melbourne, Australia. He is also the author of Twisted Tales, Volume 1 and two children's books. A Change of Heart is the first book in a planned trilogy. The father of two sons, he lives with his wife, Kristy, in South Morang, Victoria, Australia.

Printed in the United States
By Bookmasters